AUDACITY *A Novel*

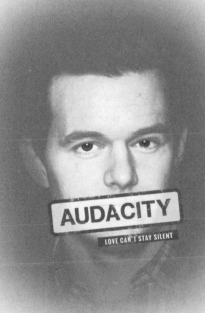

Based on the movie by
RAY **COMFORT**

Novelization by
JULIA **ZWAYNE**

genesis
PUBLISHING GROUP

Audacity: A Novel

Published by
Genesis Publishing Group
2002 Skyline Place
Bartlesville, OK 74006
www.genesis-group.net

Edited by Lynn Copeland

Cover illustration by Brad Snow

Photos by Carol Scott, CJ-Studio.com

Chapter illustrations by Manuel Brambila

Cover layout, page design, and production by Genesis Group

ISBN 978-1-933591-23-0 (pbk.)
ISBN 978-1-933591-24-7 (e-book)

Printed in the United States of America

See **www.AudacityMovie.com** to watch "Audacity" and find details on related resources.

To all who love enough to not stay silent,
and to all those who will listen

CHAPTER ONE

"Give me your money, or I'll put a bullet in your kid's brain!"

With every fiber of his being, Peter wanted to move. He longed to throw himself in front of his mother and fling the hateful attacker to the floor. To rebel against this false authority, this intruder who claimed power.

But underneath his desire to fight stood a mere boy of eleven years, robbed of all courage, strength, and resolve. Like a cornered animal, unable to flee, he gazed down the barrel of the gun and into the eyes of his predator.

The man's face drew nearer to his own. The wild, bloodshot eyes penetrated Peter's very being, piercing his heart and leaving a scar that would never fade.

Peter's grasp tightened on his mother's arm. Her skin felt cool and clammy.

"Did you hear me?" the robber hissed, flooding Peter's face with foul breath.

The handful of others in the bank remained frozen in place. To these country folks, living in a small town where nothing unpredictable ever happened, the world seemed to come to a stop. Stark terror hung in the air. The banker stood behind the counter like carved stone, his hands extended above his head.

Peter and his mother had come to the bank to cash a check. The local grocery store wouldn't accept anything but cash, so the bank was the first stop on their list of errands. With money in hand, she turned from the counter, taking a step toward the exit as she fumbled with her purse.

Peter and his mother never made it to the door. The stranger, who had walked in unnoticed, stunned the entire room by revealing his gun and shouting for everyone to stay put.

After ransacking the small building, the thief had a large bag full of money, and Peter's mother was his last victim before he took off with his booty.

Peter dared to glance at his mother, who had not yet said a word. It was pure shock and an awareness of the robber's unpredictable nature that kept her paralyzed.

The thief lunged forward and latched his hand onto the back of Peter's neck in a vise-like grip. He brought his weapon forward, pressing the cold muzzle against Peter's forehead. "Goodbye," he whispered to his prey.

Every muscle in Peter's body tightened as terror clawed at his heart. He could feel only one thing.

The icy metal against his skin.

And he could see only one thing.

The icy eyes of his soon-to-be murderer.

Time stopped. The world blackened. Peter's breathing slowed; his body went limp. His heart, which had been threatening to burst through his chest, now nearly stopped altogether.

Goodbye.

"STOP!"

The blackness disappeared in a rush, and the world—in all its color and terror—snapped back into place. Peter's vision was restored, and a sudden alertness hit him like a slap across the face. He craned his neck to see a trembling woman, holding out her hand in the madman's direction.

"Get your hands off my son!" his mother demanded. "You can take my money! Just get out of here!"

The man's grip loosened, but he didn't release Peter altogether. Leaning in the direction of the mother, he reached for the cash in her hand.

"No! Let go of my son first!" she exclaimed with surprising boldness.

The thief had lost enough precious time. He needed to make a run for it.

He released Peter so abruptly that the boy had no time to react. His weakened legs gave way beneath him, and he dropped to the floor like a sack of flour.

Finally satisfied, the robber took his leave. Peter watched him go, deaf to the wailing sobs of his mother as she knelt down beside him and clutched him to herself. His forehead tingled, still cold from the gun's touch.

The invisible wound across his heart burned within him. An iciness crept into his being as the fleeing man disappeared from his sight. Was the man a drug addict? A wanted criminal? Peter never knew who he was, nor would he ever see him again.

After a long moment, the people in the bank seemed to let out their collective breath at once. They looked at each other incredulous, not quite knowing how to react. Some even laughed with relief. They had been spared.

But the small eleven-year-old boy, sprawled on the floor of the little bank in the Midwest, would never be the same.

———

In a small, charming restaurant, two young women had stopped for a bite to eat after work and were seated in a booth, conversing casually. "So, I've noticed you've been talking with the new guy at work. Peter, right?" asked Hailey, the dark-haired woman, as she stirred her coffee.

"Yeah, we actually went to high school together," answered Diana. "He used to race bikes."

"Motorcycles?"

Diana smiled and shook her head. "No, bicycles. Like Lance Armstrong."

"Oh, cool," Hailey said, looking up with more interest. "He must really like his job then. He's doing bike deliveries, right?"

"Yep. He's like a mailman on wheels." Diana chuckled, taking a sip of her iced tea.

"I've also noticed that he's been hanging around with the guy who sounds like the Crocodile Hunter."

"Yeah, that's Ben. He's Peter's buddy. He grew up in Australia. I'm actually starting to become good friends with both of them. Because our departments overlap, we see quite a bit of each other at the office. Ben moonlights as a comedian. The guy is hilarious!" She suddenly paused, her eyes widening in shock. "Ben! Oh no!" she gasped, clapping her hand over her mouth.

"What?" Hailey set her mug down, alarmed.

"I'm such a dope, Hailey!" Diana pressed her palm against her forehead and rolled her eyes. "Ben's show was tonight and I totally forgot about it! He was especially getting on me about going to this one, and I promised I would!" She let out an enormous sigh of frustration.

Hailey couldn't suppress a smirk. "Oooh, busted! He's not going to let you live this one down." She giggled into her coffee mug as she took another sip.

"I know! I can't believe I forgot! I'd better text him right away." Diana whipped out her phone and began dictating her text in an Australian accent. "I'm so sorry. I beg your forgiveness." Both girls broke into laughter.

"So were you and Peter good friends in high school?" Hailey inquired after a slight pause.

"Actually, no, not at all," Diana replied. "We didn't even really know each other. He was just in one of my classes. He was pretty popular—kind of known for being a partier. He seems different now, though. Something about him has changed . . . but I'm not exactly sure what it is."

Hailey shrugged. "People change."

"Yeah," Diana added thoughtfully. "They definitely do."

Quiet laughter and excited murmurs rippled through the audience as anticipation filled the room.

A young man in his twenties, seated in the crowd, craned his neck over the fidgeting, whispering people to catch a glimpse of the stage. Vacant and dark, it evoked an air of impatience from the crowd.

Peter ran his fingers through his mop of brown hair, glancing down at his watch. *Any minute now*, he thought. Every seat in the place was filled, and he was as eager as anyone for the night to begin.

Finally, a lone light flickered on, partially illumining the stage. A hush descended on the audience, like a blanket settling over the entire room.

A figure, unidentifiable, stepped onto the stage. The shadows kept his face safely hidden. He stood for a moment in silence, a mere silhouette.

"The time has come for change," began an authoritative voice. "For far too long in this country, too many of us have been afraid to speak up about the things that matter."

Heads turned, as several people in the crowd exchanged surprised glances with each other. Was —was that the voice of President Barack Obama? It sounded identical, a flawless representation.

"Regardless of our apprehension, the time to speak is now."

The mysterious figure stepped forward, allowing the spotlight to flood over him, revealing his identity. A tall white man, good-looking with a stubble beard, stood before them.

Peter grinned as he watched his long-time friend up there, performing for hundreds of people at the crowded comedy club. He was proud of him.

Several titters and chuckles echoed through the room from amused audience members. This guy was good, the imitation perfect. Others just stared in fascination, eager for him to go on.

"The time for change is now!" the young man continued, in the articulate tone of the president. "Together, we can change American football to rugby. Helmets are for wimps!"

Peter's eyes grew big. Ouch. He turned to catch the reaction of the audience.

"Boo! Not funny!"

But the place roared with laughter. They couldn't help it.

"All right. Sorry." The voice of Obama melted into an Australian accent, the comedian's real voice. Now the crowd didn't need an explanation for the insult. "Joking about the president, okay. Joking about football, not allowed. My bad."

A wave of laughter rippled through the audience again. This guy was hard not to like.

Peter laughed along with them. He clapped for Ben Price, a man he looked up to for his boldness and the ability to entertain people and bring them joy. *What a guy*, he thought, grinning from ear to ear.

His friend was on a roll. "I love Arnold Schwarzenegger. He's done a movie recently with Sylvester Stallone. Stallone calls him and says, 'You know, I'm wondering, you know, would you like a cameo in my latest movie?' And Arnie says, 'I'm too busy for a cameo. But how about a small part?'"

As Ben continued his impersonations, his talent was increasingly evident. His imitation of various actors, famous characters, and well-known celebrities made for an excellent performance.

The lively show finally came to an end. Peter joined in the heartfelt applause as Ben wrapped up the night with a final farewell to his audience.

Peter stayed seated, as one by one the crowd dispersed and trickled out of the comedy club. He waited for the room to empty before heading backstage.

"I'm here for an autograph...," Peter said, clapping slowly as he approached his friend.

"Thank you, man."

"Not yours."

"Ahh." Ben grinned as he packed up his laptop and held it out to Peter. "Take my bag."

"No, no. I'm union, I'd better not," Peter quipped. As they headed for the exit, he continued. "Really, man, you did great, as always. I mean, everyone was laughing and having an amazing time. But I thought they were going to waterboard you over the rugby thing," Peter commented, smirking.

"Yeah, I know. It was a risk, a risk I was willing to take."

"No risk, no reward, huh?"

Ben let out a hearty laugh, and Peter joined in.

When the two friends were together, the real world faded into the background as their lighthearted friendship took center stage. For them, the comedy show never ended. They always had something to laugh about.

After meeting at a comedy workshop, the

two of them hit it off immediately and became good friends, never ceasing to enjoy each other's company. Ben had even found a position for Peter at his workplace. Also, their friendship had hit a deeper level because of Peter's recent conversion to Christianity. They now shared the same beliefs and convictions.

"So, when are you going to step onto the stage?"

Peter blinked.

Ben might as well have dumped a glass of cold water on him.

"Me? I, uh...next week. Oh, never, that's what I meant. Never, yeah." Just thinking about it made his stomach clench in knots. A nerve-wracking anxiety stole over him anytime he talked in front of even a few people, much less an entire crowd.

"No, seriously, you've got some great material," Ben persisted. "I think you're ready."

"Yeah, but you laugh at anything." Peter gave him a knowing look.

"True." Ben grinned. "So when are you going to do it so I can laugh at you?"

"Well, what do I owe you for that inspiration, Tony Robbins?"

"Seriously, I just want to be the first to throw something at you."

Peter rolled his eyes. "You know who liked that joke? Nobody."

Both of them laughed once again, but inside, Peter mulled over the possibility of stepping onto the stage. He knew it would take a miracle for that to happen. Though he had a strong interest in stand-up comedy, and a desire to make others laugh, a deep fear in his heart hindered him.

Fear had been pursuing him ever since he was a boy. A leech that clung to his being, it sucked away every ounce of boldness he possessed. A mere acquaintance in the beginning, it now tried at every circumstance to claim him altogether.

And one day, if Peter wasn't careful, fear would become his master.

CHAPTER TWO

Peter lay under the covers in the dimness of his bedroom, his eyelids heavy as he flipped through the television channels. Cooking contest. Talk show. Nature channel. Crime show. He yawned, lingering on each channel for only a few seconds before moving on to the next.

After watching a scene of a South American man searching for a rare beetle in the Amazon, Peter skipped ahead once again, feeling a wave of fatigue wash over him.

"For some, the legalization of gay marriage is good news, while others find it difficult to grasp," intoned the reporter on a local news show. "Regardless of what anyone thinks about the issue, gay marriage has become a present-day reality that is spreading across America. Soon, to one degree or another, each of us will have to respond in our own way to this current cultural revolution."

Peter, in his sleepy state, tried to mull over the report in his muddled brain. Gay marriage had become a controversial issue over the past few years, but he never seemed to think about it in depth. Perhaps he would look into the subject more. Peter yawned again and turned off the TV.

<hr />

Removing the pot from the coffee maker, Peter set his empty mug on the counter and poured steaming hot coffee into it. The rich aroma wafted into the air. Lifting the mug to his nose, he inhaled deeply before bringing the cup to his lips.

After a long sip, Peter grabbed a muffin from the coffee station and headed for the sofa on the other side of the room. As he sank into the softness of the couch, he glanced around the empty break room, listening to the sounds of bustling activity echoing from the halls: ringing phones, hurried footsteps, buzzing conversation.

The busy company Peter worked for was Cybix Creative, a high-tech company in the Los Angeles area, where employees recovered data from damaged hard drives. Recovered lost data could sometimes be worth tens, or hundreds, of thousands of dollars, and Cybix promised the fastest recovery in the state—guaranteed. Whether the loss involved crucial business data, sensitive political information, legal documents for court cases, or an author's half-finished manuscript, it was all vital to the owners. So when a client stated a drop-dead time that they needed the data on-hand, it had to be delivered on time. More than one delivery person has lost his job when a deadline was missed.

That's where Peter came in. He delivered these time-sensitive packages by bike, enabling him to weave around traffic in the often grid-locked streets. It proved to be a stressful job, but one that Peter was happy to tackle. It had been a couple of months since Peter had been hired, and he was grateful that Ben had recommended him for the job. Bike racing had been a long-time passion of his, so it was enjoyable for him to get paid to do something that he loved, and the deliveries kept him hopping most of the day.

As a slim, pretty, young woman entered the break room, Peter glanced up and smiled at his coworker. "Hey, Diana."

Diana, heading for the coffee station, smiled in return. "Oh, hi, Peter! I thought you'd left already. When is your first delivery?"

"Pretty soon. I'm still trying to wake up." As if on cue, a big yawn escaped him.

Diana took a seat on the large L-shaped sectional wrapped around the coffee table, sitting on the small section to Peter's right. The sweet-natured young lady, with auburn hair framing a sharp-featured face, set her own coffee mug on the table and placed a muffin beside it.

Diana appeared friendly and confident, but, like Peter, she too had hidden scars from her past. Her father had been physically abusive since the time she was five, and her parents' loveless marriage ended when she was only ten years old, leaving her feeling confused and abandoned. Although Diana's mother had tried to be a loving and supportive parent in those following years, she barely had time to pour into her three children as she struggled to make ends meet.

Her mother didn't remarry, so Diana never knew the genuine love of a father—only the painful memories of her own father, who had no interest in being a part of their lives after the divorce. And the feeling was mutual. *Who needs him*, Diana would tell herself, whenever she felt a twinge of sorrow at being fatherless. At least Diana and her older brother and sister had each other to count on.

Now an accomplished young woman in her twenties, working in the financial department at Cybix Creative, she purposed to never let her insecurity show, but concealed it with an air of confidence.

"So, how was Ben's show?" she inquired, her eyes bright with interest. "It was last night, right? No wonder you're tired."

"Oh, it was great. They loved him." Peter couldn't help grinning, reliving the comedy club experience of the night before.

"Now, you do that too, right?" she probed, her expression betraying her curiosity. "Ben says you're pretty good. I'm surprised you've never told me about it."

Peter couldn't help laughing. "Really? He said that?"

"Yeah, he mentioned it the other day."

Peter shook his head. "Well, I wouldn't say that."

"Can you do one?" Diana leaned forward, her hazel eyes lighting up with anticipation.

Peter brushed it off. "No, no, no, no." He took a bite of his muffin.

"Come on."

"Nooo."

"Oh, come on, Peter!" Diana persisted. "Just do a little one! No one's here," she whispered conspiratorially, gesturing around the room. "Please?"

Peter knew if he didn't give her what she wanted, he would never hear the end of it. The expectation in her face finally nudged him into giving in.

"I'm really not very good," he warned her again.

"That's okay."

"All right." He drew in a deep breath, then slowly exhaled. "Okay, here goes."

Diana grinned as she eagerly waited for him to begin.

"You familiar with Russell Crowe—the crazy guy who throws phones at people?" Peter asked.

Her eyes rolled. "Yes, of course!"

Peter geared himself to present the impersonation, but his tongue felt as if it were caught in a mousetrap. His heart began to quicken, and his hands grew clammy. *Come on, you chicken,* his mind screeched at him as fear gripped his heart.

With his gaze rooted on the floor, he now had the pattern of the rug memorized. He knew, as he grew more and more embarrassed, that he would have to say something before he was completely humiliated.

"I can't do him," Peter finally said, defeated.

"Oh, come *on!*"

"I can't do him, but I got a mean Popeye. I got a *mean* Popeye."

"Wow," Diana said exasperated.

Just then the alarm on Peter's phone went off. He snatched at the distraction, and picking up his phone, he turned off the alarm. "I've got to get going pretty soon," he said.

To his surprise, Diana let the whole impersonation thing drop.

"Are you going to be on time this time?" Diana teased, the corners of her mouth lifting ever so slightly.

Peter felt the jab of her question. Just last week, he had been late while delivering an important package. His boss had called him into his office after the incident, and Peter had escaped losing his job by a hair. It was a close call. He cringed just thinking about it.

"I'd better," he replied. "I can't believe they're giving me another chance."

"Everyone makes mistakes."

"That's true. How many times have you run out of gas?" Now it was Peter's turn to make a good-natured jab at her.

Diana was known around the office as one who usually waited to fill her gas tank until it pretty much ran empty. "Come on, guys," she would quip. "Doesn't 'E' mean 'Enough'?"

"Shut up." Diana tried to glare at him, but a slowly spreading smile won out.

"Was it three or four?"

"No, shut up, shut up."

"Seven?" Peter shook his head, laughing.

"No. It was *once*."

"Well, who's keeping count?"

"You," Diana mumbled under her breath.

As Diana took another sip of her coffee, Peter glanced down at his watch. He had a few minutes to spare. Pulling out his iPad, he decided he would read a couple verses of Scripture before he made his delivery run. He opened his Bible app, beginning to read where he had left off.

Diana watched him over her cup of coffee. "What are you looking at?" she asked with friendly curiosity.

"I'm reading the Bible."

A long pause followed. Peter continued to read, but became painfully aware that Diana had sobered up, and seemed to be deep in thought.

"Oh. So, you're religious?" she piped up, breaking the silence.

"Well, I'm a Christian."

"Since when?"

"Since about a year ago."

"So . . . you believe the Bible is true?"

"Yeah. Every word."

"So you read it every day, and you completely trust what it says?" Her tone had hardened, and her friendly attitude began to ebb away.

"Absolutely." Peter willed himself to remain unmoved by her change of mood. The atmosphere in the room had shifted, like a cloud moving in front of the sun without warning.

"So, do you believe in slavery?"

Peter's head snapped up in surprise. Diana had her lips pursed, with an almost accusing look.

"What do you mean?" Peter said, incredulous.

Diana rolled her eyes. "The Bible says it's okay to own slaves. Everyone knows that. So how many do you have?"

Now she was getting cocky. Peter took a deep breath, trying to steady his thoughts.

"Diana, do you really want an answer, or are you just baiting me?"

"I really want to know how you are going to justify this." Diana's breezy, easygoing mood had vanished. She sat there, coolly, waiting for him to respond.

Peter set his iPad on the coffee table, as if to buy a couple seconds to prepare himself for a response.

"I can justify it, but it will take a minute to explain. Are you okay with that?" The last thing he wanted was for Diana to be upset with him. If they talked this thing out, maybe they could leave the room without getting into a heated argument.

Diana's face softened ever so slightly. "Sure."

Peter had been troubled by a similar question when he first became a Christian, so he searched the Scriptures for an explanation. After careful study, he came to an understanding of what the Bible means when it mentions slavery.

"We tend to look at it through the eyes of American history," he began, "where Africans were kidnapped from their families, shipped like cattle to the United States, sold as slaves, and treated with terrible cruelty. Kidnapping under Hebrew law, however, was outlawed and was punishable by death. So the 'slaves' spoken of in the Bible weren't kidnapped, although some were taken and used for forced labor after a war. Instead of killing their enemies, the conquering nations would sometimes use them as slaves. The Hebrews themselves were slaves in Egypt for four hundred years. Germany and Japan used prisoners as slave labor during World War II."

Peter paused to clear his throat. Glancing at Diana, he gathered that she seemed to be mulling over his words, but wasn't quite sure what to think yet. She studied him with a piercing gaze, waiting.

His voice shook slightly, but it was too late to back out now. He continued, "But the slavery we are talking about here was different. Slaves were often called 'bond servants.' We still speak of 'bonds' nowadays. For instance, a bail bond is money put up as a guarantee that if the police let you out of jail, you'll stick around for the court case. Once that happens, they return your bond money.

"In Bible times, if someone got into debt, they could pay off that 'bond' by working as a servant, or 'slave,' for the person to whom they owed money. Nowadays, when people get into serious debt and can't pay their creditors, they're thrown into prison, costing the state billions, and no one gets paid back. So, there's slavery according to the Bible. Does that make sense?"

Diana bit her lip, hesitant to respond. Finally, she sighed and blurted, "Okay. I get it. So you answered that one." A challenging glint flickered in her eyes. "I have another that I don't think you'll be able to answer."

Peter smiled at her. "Let me give it a try."

"Do you believe that gay people should be stoned?"

Peter almost spit out his bite of muffin. "What? Of course not!"

"Well, your book says that," Diana retorted. "That's one that you're not going to get around."

Peter could feel a panicky sensation in the pit of his stomach. He scrambled for the right response, digging deep in his brain for a way to contradict her statement. "No, actually, it doesn't say that," he managed to stammer. "I was just reading yesterday in—"

"I don't want to offend you," Diana cut in, "but I have a sister who's gay. And you don't know the struggle she's been through...because of people who have told her that she's going to Hell. For what? Just loving someone?"

Peter stared at the rug again, stumped. He knew the truth. He knew what he believed. But her questions were somehow difficult for him to answer. Also, the fact that Diana was emotionally involved with this subject made it a whole lot harder.

"I...ah..."

But Diana wasn't finished. "And you have the audacity to think that she's headed for Hell!" An angry flush reddened her face. "Go on, say it. 'She's on her way to Hell.' That's what Christians believe."

Peter opened his mouth to respond, but at that moment, the alarm went off on his phone once more. He glanced at his watch. *Yikes.* If he didn't leave immediately, his job would be at stake.

Peter stood to his feet. Though he wished he could answer her questions, he was relieved at the opportunity to leave the tense situation.

"Listen, I'm sorry," he said awkwardly. "But I've got to go."

Diana made no response.

Closing his iPad, Peter exited the room without looking back.

After grabbing the delivery package and instructions, Peter gripped the handle bars of his bike and pedaled as fast as his legs would allow. The air whipped at his face as he weaved through traffic. *I'd better not be late this time!* he thought.

Diana's words echoed in the back of his mind. "And you have the audacity to think that she's headed for Hell!"

How can I make Diana understand? Peter thought with frustration. He couldn't seem to remember the key verses about homosexuality in the Bible that would be helpful to share with her. He wanted her to listen with an open mind without completely misunderstanding him.

Peter snaked his way through cars and passersby as he pedaled through the streets. He took a quick detour, cutting his way through a small park in the middle of the city. A tornado of thoughts caused his focus to waver.

All at once, a pedestrian appeared directly in front of him, in the middle of the sidewalk. The man yelled in surprise, jerking himself out of the way, just as Peter swerved to the left at the last second.

"What's your problem?!" the man yelled in shock.

"Sorry! Sorry!" Peter shouted over his shoulder, feeling terrible, but knowing that if he wasted even a moment, he could lose his job.

Just the thought gave him an extra burst of energy, and he raced up the street, trying to keep his mind off Diana.

CHAPTER THREE

With perspiration dripping down his temples, Peter parked his bike outside the large office building, unlocked his delivery package from the bike, and ran frantically through the front entrance.

He hurried past the people in the lobby and made a beeline for the elevator. "Hold it, hold it, hold it!" Peter shouted as he saw the elevator doors beginning to shut, but he made it just in time, jamming his arm into the gap and parting the doors before they closed.

Two young women stood inside. "What floor are you going to?" Peter asked them.

"Twenty-seven," one of them answered with a smile.

Seeing that they had already pressed their floor button, Peter quickly pushed "28," then stepped back. As he struggled to catch his breath, he glanced at the two girls. They were standing closely with their arms linked, laughing and whispering excitedly.

"You two look happy," Peter commented.

One of the girls, with dark hair and eyes, grinned and announced, "We're here to apply for our marriage license!"

Peter could only stare in silence. That same nervous sensation, very familiar to him, began to gnaw at his insides.

"Can you believe we're doing this?" one of the girls bubbled to the other.

"I know. It feels like a dream," her partner replied.

"Oh, did you call the florist? We should probably go there next. I feel like we have so much to do; it's going to be here before we know it."

"I know!"

Palms sweaty, Peter reached into his back pocket, his fingers closing over a booklet—a Christian gospel tract titled "Why Christianity?" In recent months, Peter had begun carrying tracts with him wherever he went. He had a deep desire to share the gospel with others, so he decided that passing out tracts was a great way to do it. With his gaze fixed on the chattering girls, Peter tried to muster the courage to simply whip out the tract and hand it to them; it would all be over in a matter of seconds. But that monster called fear kept Peter's hand glued inside his pocket. No matter what his conscience screamed at him, his body wouldn't let him move.

"That's a cool bag," said the dark-haired girl, eyeing the delivery satchel slung over Peter's shoulder. "Are you a bike messenger?"

"Uh, yeah. Yeah."

"So...what's your message?"

"Hah. No, actually...I'm more of a bike delivery person," Peter said with an awkward laugh. "I, uh, I don't deliver bikes. I guess 'bike messenger' sounds better than 'bike delivery person.'" As he stammered his reply, he pushed the tract back into the depths of his pocket.

The elevator doors slid open, ending the conversation. Peter was mad at himself for letting fear get the best of him—again.

"Well, have a nice day," the brunette said.

"Yeah, you too."

With cordial smiles, the young women exited the elevator, walking down the hallway hand in hand.

As the couple reached the end of the hall, an older man watched them pass by, his brows furrowed with a look of irritation on his features. He walked away, shaking his head in disgust.

Moments after the girls left, the elevator doors began to close. Peter glanced at his watch. He had barely a few minutes left before he had to deliver the package.

The elevator was still and silent. Peter looked up, noticing for the first time that the doors hadn't shut completely. He stared through the gap between the doors, confused. Nothing was happening. The elevator hadn't budged.

With a sigh of frustration, Peter pushed the button again. Nothing. The elevator made no response.

Suddenly, with a sickening jolt, the floor disappeared under Peter's feet. The air left his lungs as the elevator dropped with a loud metallic clang. Knocked to the floor, Peter didn't realize he had his eyes closed tightly until he opened them. He stood to his feet and examined his surroundings.

The elevator had dropped only about three feet, and no further.

While waiting for his heartbeat to return to normal, Peter attempted to part the doors, but to no avail.

Like the slow bubbling of soup steaming in a pot, panic began to rise within him. Taking a deep breath to steady himself, he stepped to the keypad and pushed the Call button for the emergency operator. He didn't dare mess with any of the other buttons, fearful that the elevator might drop even further.

"Can I help you?" a man's voice inquired.

"Yeah, I'm stuck in the elevator. The doors won't open and I'm halfway down the floor," Peter answered anxiously.

"Okay, one moment, please," the operator replied, calm and collected. Peter, given his sense of urgency, couldn't decide whether the man's calmness was reassuring or irritating.

Peter pressed his forehead against the cold metal wall, taking deep breaths and trying not to lose it. Not only was he in a dangerous predicament, but the time was quickly ebbing away.

The man's voice returned, jolting him to his senses.

"There's been a serious malfunction. Very carefully, you need to get out of the elevator. Try pressing the Door Open button."

Peter pressed the button and nothing happened. Trying not to panic, he said, "It's not working. It's not doing anything. It won't open. I mean, the doors are open, but only slightly."

"Hang on, I'm entering a code." After a pause, the operator instructed him, "Okay, now try pushing the doors open."

A surge of adrenaline catapulted Peter into action. Following the operator's directions, he placed his hands on both doors and pushed them apart as hard as he could. They creaked open. Holding onto the doors, Peter managed to pull himself up and squeeze through the opening.

Now outside of the elevator, he didn't have time to relish that moment of freedom. Bending down so the operator could hear him, he called into the elevator, "All right, I'm out now. Thanks."

"Good," came the voice from inside. "Now I need you to wait outside the door, and stop anyone from getting into the elevator until I get a technician on site."

Panic bubbled up inside him again, but this time with greater force. "What? No, no, no. I can't do that!" Peter argued. "I have a very important delivery. I have to leave now."

A sudden straining and creaking sound came from the elevator shaft. Peter could've sworn he heard cables twanging, as if they were on the brink of snapping.

"You can't leave." The operator's voice was tight with panic. *"Someone could die!"*

"I'll figure something out. I can't be late!"

"No! You can't leave!" the operator protested, his voice almost a shout. "This is serious. You need to warn…"

Suddenly, the doors closed shut, cutting off his communication with the operator.

Peter stood there, alone in an empty hallway. He frantically looked from right to left, trying to find an employee, a janitor, a customer—anyone. "Hello? I need help! Can anybody help me?" he yelled in desperation.

With trembling hands, he fumbled through his delivery bag and found a Sharpie and a piece of paper. Taking a stick of gum from his pocket, he popped it into his mouth, chewing furiously as he scribbled a note:

Danger! Broken elevator!
DO NOT ENTER!

Then he took the gum out of his mouth and used it to stick the sign to the elevator door.

Digging into his bag again, he pulled out the package and examined the label. "Floor 28 ...okay," he muttered. "What suite number?" He scanned the package: 2810. "Got it." With the number now in mind, he was about to look for the stairwell.

"What's going on here?"

Peter jerked his head up in surprise. An older gentleman stood in front of him, concern and bewilderment on his face.

"Hey!" Relieved to find someone to stand guard while he completed his delivery, Peter blurted out, "Listen, you gotta stay and watch this elevator for me. It's broken, and could fall if any weight is put on it. So just stay here and make sure no one gets on!"

The man gave him a hesitant nod, but Peter barely acknowledged it. "I'll be right back. I'll be right back!" he yelled as he raced down the hallway, package in hand. He would not allow another wasted moment to pass.

As the man watched him go, female voices drifted from the other end of the hallway. After peering in that direction for several seconds, the man could hear the lesbian couple he had seen earlier chatting excitedly about their marriage license and plans for their upcoming wedding. They left the office behind, and came walking down the hall in the man's direction— headed for the elevator.

That same look of disgust came over his face. The young women were so preoccupied with their conversation that they hadn't seen him yet. A malicious expression suddenly flickered in his eyes. With one last glance at the girls, he reached out, ripped Peter's sign off of the elevator, crushed it in his hand, and casually walked away.

Seconds later, the young women reached the elevator. The old man, with a sneer of satisfaction, glanced over his shoulder as he watched them enter. Then he left the scene, simply an innocent bystander.

At that moment, Peter reentered the hallway, coming back as promised to wait for the repair technician. Like the zoom lens on a camera, his vision tunneled to the elevator—just in time to see the elevator doors shut behind the women.

As if catapulted by a cannon, he flew down the hallway at a speed he never knew he possessed. A creaking and groaning, along with the snapping of cables, echoed through the hall. Haunting screams joined the sickening sounds.

Peter reached the elevator, falling to his knees and slamming his fists against the doors. A cry of horror escaped his lips in one resounding, "*Noo-o-o-o!*" followed by a deafening crash.

As he screamed in his terror and guilt, a swirling blackness swallowed him whole, smothering all sound and vision.

And then a light penetrated the darkness. With a choking gasp, Peter sat up, his forehead drenched in sweat. He blinked several times, trying to gauge his surroundings as his heart hammered in his chest.

He was in his bedroom, sitting up in bed.

It had all been a nightmare.

CHAPTER FOUR

⟡

Dazed, several minutes passed before Peter could shake off the shock of the dream and climb out of bed. He made his way to the kitchen and began to make himself a cup of coffee.

After he was settled at the table, he opened his laptop and went to the Internet. With the nightmare fresh in his mind, he typed into the search bar "How to witness to a homosexual." He was puzzled about why his coworker was in his dream, but regardless, he realized he needed to be ready to address this topic so his fears wouldn't keep him tongue-tied.

Numerous results popped up, but one in particular stood out to him. He clicked the link, and a video came up of a man interviewing people on the street. After watching a minute, Peter discovered that the man was asking individuals their opinions on homosexuality. Curious, Peter continued to watch.

He noticed that each of the interviews started with a question about gay marriage. Did people support it? Almost everyone did. The answers intrigued Peter, because he had noticed a huge cultural shift in the last few years. It was as though, as a Christian, he was standing on the outside of the culture, looking in.

As several interviews took place, another key question asked was whether people are born gay. The most common answer, from both homosexuals and heterosexuals, was yes. Surprisingly, some who were gay answered no. That was a question Peter had often wondered about.

The man with the microphone would then ask, "Do you think people are born with the tendency to commit adultery? Or to fornicate?"

Most of those interviewed said, "No."

"Well, I was born with those tendencies," the interviewer insisted. "Everyone is born with the desire to do whatever they want to do, even though it's wrong. I knew fornication was wrong, but I still wanted to do it. I was born like that! I couldn't help it. The desires overtook me. But that doesn't make it right."

The responses jumped out at Peter as he watched. *That's a very good argument*, he thought.

As remnants of his nightmare floated in the back of his thoughts, he continued to watch the video in fascination, hoping he could gather some helpful insights.

Peter took a long sip of his coffee, absentmindedly peeking over his shoulder at the two young women in the break room. Diana was seated at a table, chatting with her friend Hailey.

"I couldn't believe how inexpensive it was, and it's the same as the one we saw at the mall the other day," Diana was saying, gesturing to the shirt she was wearing.

"It looks so cute on you!" Hailey said in admiration. She glanced at the clock on the wall. "Oh, I gotta go. I'll talk to you later." The two exchanged a smile, and Hailey left the room.

Peter, who had been waiting around for Hailey to leave, seized the moment. Moving over to the table, he set his coffee mug down and said with a teasing glint in his eye, "That shirt looks so-o-o cute on you."

"Stop, you are such a creeper." Diana laughed and shook her head at him as he sat down across from her. Peter chuckled, but quickly became serious. He had something on his mind and he couldn't hold it in much longer.

"Hey, Diana," he began, trying to act casual. "This is going to sound strange...but do you have a sister?"

"Yeah, I do," she replied with a smile, a bit surprised at the question.

Peter paused, cringing as the next words formed on his lips. "Is she . . . gay?"

Diana's eyes widened, and her eyebrows arched in confusion. "No. Why do you ask?"

"Well . . . ," he said hesitantly, "I had a dream last night . . ."

"About my sister?" Diana said perplexed. "She's married, with kids!"

Not sure what to make of his dream, Peter was silent for a moment. Finally, he asked, "Do you mind if I ask you another question?"

"Sure, go ahead."

Peter cleared his throat. "What do you think of gay marriage?"

"Well . . ." Diana paused in thought. "I think that people who love each other should have the right to get married. Don't you?"

Peter had already geared himself for the conversation, but he felt nervous nonetheless. "I think there's more to it than that. I'm a Christian, and the Bible says—"

"The Bible says a lot of things," Diana interjected, rolling her eyes. "I mean, doesn't it say that God sends gay people to Hell?"

"You're missing the point. Jesus came to save people from Hell—"

"Don't get me wrong. I believe in God," Diana interrupted again. "It's just that my God doesn't damn people to Hell just because they're different."

Peter reached into his bag and pulled out his iPad. Setting it on the table, he said, "Let me show you something. It's a video of a Christian talking with a gay couple."

"I'd really rather not," Diana said with a frown, as Peter pulled up the video on his iPad. "These people are always so condescending and judgmental. I mean, why is the Bible so against sex?"

Peter laughed in spite of the situation. "The Bible isn't against sex. The whole thing starts with God telling two naked people to have sex! They're literally halfway home."

Diana couldn't help laughing along with him. The tension began to clear, and she could feel the conversation lighten up a bit.

"I've never really thought of it like that," she admitted.

"And I know there are psychos out there holding up hateful signs about gay people," Peter continued. "But most Christians aren't like that. That's not even Christian! Just watch the ending of the video, and then if you're open, maybe I could show you the whole thing."

Peter forwarded the video to the last few seconds. It was the same clip he had been watching earlier that morning. In this scene, the Christian man was just wrapping up the conversation with the lesbian couple.

"Is there anything else you'd like to say?" he asked them.

"No, thank you," one of the girls responded pleasantly.

"You're all finished?"

"Yep! All good!" Both girls were smiling, and seemed to be on good terms with the man who was interviewing them.

"Thank you for being so kind and understanding, and not very judgmental about this," the other girl said with sincere gratitude.

The video ended, and Peter glanced at Diana to see her response. She was silent for a moment, seemingly debating within herself. Finally, with a sigh and another eye-roll, she said, "Fine. You can show me the rest." Peter rejoiced inwardly that she had agreed.

Peter started the three-minute video from the beginning as they watched it together. He hoped they would be able to view the brief clip without distractions from others entering the break room. It was awkward enough without having to explain to someone else what they were watching.

Throughout the clip, the man spoke with several individuals, interviewing them about their views on homosexuality. In one conversation, a lesbian was asked if she believed in God.

"Yes, I believe in God," she affirmed.

He asked a second question. "So what does God think about homosexuality?"

"I think God is okay with homosexuality."

Others replied, "God wants people to be happy," or "He frowns upon it, but He still loves me at the end of the day, since we're all sinners."

At one point in the video, an individual was asked to read 1 Corinthians 6:9,10: "Do not be deceived. Neither fornicators, nor idolaters, nor adulterers, nor homosexuals, nor sodomites, nor thieves...will inherit the kingdom of God."

The Christian man explained that some churches teach that homosexuals *can* enter the kingdom of Heaven. "They teach that adulterers and fornicators can't, but they claim that gays can enter—homosexuals get a free pass. That's a huge betrayal."

"I accepted Jesus into my heart, and that's all I need," one of the lesbian girls stated, trying to justify herself.

"No," the man said gently. "You need to repent, turn from all sin. No lying, stealing, adultery, fornication, homosexuality. You have to turn from all sin."

Peter studied Diana as she watched the video with genuine interest. He hoped she would listen closely as the video's message took another turn.

The Christian interviewer moved into an even deeper subject. "So what about you? If you were to die today, where would you go? Do you believe in an afterlife?"

The interviewees gave their various opinions, and asked if they thought they were a good person, most said yes.

"Do you think you'll go to Heaven or Hell when you die?"

While the majority believed they would go to Heaven, one man answered candidly: "If I don't repent of my homosexuality, I will most definitely go to Hell."

The interviewer began to ask a series of more personal questions—whether the individuals had ever broken any of the Ten Commandments, God's moral Law.

"Have you ever told a lie? Have you ever stolen anything?"

"Yes."

"Jesus said if you look at a woman to lust for her, you've already committed adultery with her in your heart. Have you ever looked at someone with lust? Have you ever used God's name in vain?"

Diana scrutinized the screen in concentration, fascinated as the man questioned the people with a kind and loving attitude, yet he wasn't afraid to be direct and personal. Each individual in turn admitted their guilt, yet none were offended by the gentle approach. This was not at all the condescending attitude Diana had expected of Christians.

The video concluded with one last statement.

"God can let you live forever because of what Jesus did on the cross, suffering and dying for the sin of the world. Jesus paid your fine through His life's blood, then He rose from the dead and defeated death. And what you have to do is repent—turn from your sins—and trust in Him. The minute you do that, God will dismiss your case. He'll forgive your sins, and legally grant you everlasting life. That's the good news of the gospel."

When the video ended, Diana asked, "Can I go back a bit?" Peter nodded, and Diana went back to the scene where one of the lesbians said, "I accepted Jesus into my heart."

"They were Christians," Diana said, her brow furrowing as she looked at Peter in bewilderment.

"A lot of people make a profession of faith in Christ, but they continue to live however they want to live. It's called self-deception when we do that."

Diana only nodded, dropping her gaze and tracing her finger along the table, deep in thought.

Peter glanced at his watch. "I have to get going. Thanks for letting me talk to you about this." He stood and began to pack up his iPad, then remembered something. "Hey, Ben has a show tonight. You should come."

"Yeah, sure." Diana attempted to smile, but her demeanor hinted that something was wrong. "Hey... before you go, I just have a quick favor to ask."

Peter detected the somberness in her voice, so he sat down again and gave her his full attention.

Diana drew a deep breath before speaking. "My brother, Eric, has really bad cancer. He's dying, and he has a wife and three beautiful kids." Her lip began to quiver and her voice cracked with emotion. She looked up at the ceiling in an effort to hold in the tears. "Why is this happening? What did he do to deserve this?"

Despite her attempt not to cry, a tear escaped and trickled down her cheek. "I'm so…so angry at God."

Peter's heart filled with compassion as he saw the pain in Diana's eyes. Amid the hurt and devastation over her brother's cancer, Peter sensed her inner turmoil, and he wished that he could say something to make her feel better. She wasn't alone in blaming God for the suffering she'd seen, but Peter was speechless about how to answer her. He hoped to at least be a good friend to her. To be someone she could trust.

Looking straight into her eyes, he said with genuine concern, "I'm really sorry this is happening. But I will definitely be praying for him."

"Thank you," she whispered gratefully, wiping the tear from her face.

Peter gave her a gentle, loving smile, then quietly left the room.

CHAPTER FIVE

Tap, tap, tap. Ben drummed his fingers on the steering wheel, humming a random tune under his breath as he kept his eyes on the traffic light. After a long week of handling customer calls in the Communications department, he was always happy that Cybix closed at noon on Fridays. Aside from the enjoyment of talking with people, that was another great reason he loved his job. Today he was looking forward to spending the afternoon relaxing, rehearsing, and maybe getting in a little snooze so he would be refreshed before heading out again.

While Ben waited for the light to turn green, he thought about his show coming up that evening, and the new impersonations he was eager to test out. He was continually looking around him for inspiration, trying to think of fresh material to throw into the gig. As his gaze wandered to the vehicle in front of him, he noticed a strange symbol on the back window of the Honda. It appeared to be some kind of skull-faced demon.

Just then, the light turned green. Ben eased his foot off of the brake, preparing to cross the intersection. The Honda accelerated quickly, reaching the middle of the intersection just as the roar of an engine pierced the air. A fraction of a second later, a large, black SUV, attempting to make it through the light, barreled through the intersection from the left—headed straight for the Honda.

An earsplitting explosion blasted through the air, as if a pack of lit dynamite had been thrown into the middle of the intersection. Shards of glass flew skyward. The Honda did a 360, spiraling across the intersection like a toy car spun across a table.

Ben smashed his foot against the brake as screeching tires echoed all around him. He shoved open his car door, his muscles weak and shaky, stumbling in the direction of the collision.

Ben didn't stop to see who was there, or what was happening around him. He ran blindly to what was left of the Honda. The car lay crumpled on the far side of the intersection, a pathetic pile of metal. Ben made it there before anyone else, as others rushed to check on the driver of the SUV.

Car doors slammed, footsteps pounded. Ben, deaf to the unraveling chaos, focused on getting the man out. The driver's door, which had taken the direct impact, was completely crushed, so he ran around to the passenger door and yanked it open.

A young man lay limp and bloodied in what was left of the driver's seat. With shaking hands, Ben unbuckled the unconscious man, gathered him in his arms, and lifted him out of the car.

Ben gently laid the injured man on the sidewalk, supporting the man's head with his arm. *Was he still breathing?* Praying the young man was still alive, Ben carefully examined him, trying to determine his condition.

He had a slight build and appeared to be just out of his teens. His head, bruised and bloody, was severely injured, and blood was oozing from the side of his mouth.

As people began to crowd in from every side, trying to catch a glimpse of the victim, Ben shouted, "Stay back!" and motioned for them to give the man some space. "Has anyone called 911?"

"Yes!" a young lady declared, standing near-by. "The paramedics are on their way."

A gurgling cough snapped Ben's attention back to the young man in his arms. He seemed to be gaining consciousness. Blood continued to pour from his wounds, soaking his clothes. Ben could only cradle him, waiting for the ambulance to arrive.

As the man lay limply against Ben's arm, too weak to move, to Ben's shock, he began to speak.

"Am I dying?" he slurred, his eyes clouded with pain.

Ben opened his mouth to respond, but the man wasn't finished.

"I'm afraid to die," he rasped. As a cough wracked his frame once again, a look of dark terror crossed his features. "I'm so scared..."

Ben tried to reassure him. "It's okay. You don't need to talk. The ambulance will be here in a few minutes."

Though he was never one to be at a loss for words, Ben was completely unprepared for something like this and was totally out of his element here. He groped for the right words to say. "If—if you know that you're a sinner," he stammered, "you just need to call on Jesus, and God will give you eternal life."

The man seemed to comprehend; he nodded weakly as Ben spoke.

Ben continued to share with him, trying to keep it brief, as he was unsure of how much longer the man had to live. "Christ offers salvation as a free gift. He took our punishment for us by dying on the cross. There's nothing you can do but receive that gift and give your life to Jesus through repentance and trusting in Him."

Ben then placed his hands on the trembling young man, praying that the Lord would save him, that He would give him assurance of everlasting life. The man nodded, tears streaking his blood-caked face, as Ben prayed.

Grasping Ben's hand, he whispered, "Thank you. Tell my mom...I'm sorry...and I love her."

Shudders began to wrack his body, yet a look of peace inexplicably crossed his face. The man sucked in his breath, then let it rattle and drain out of his lungs. He didn't breathe again.

The body went limp, but the grasp on Ben's hand was not released. Ben had to pry the fingers loose to free himself of the man's death-grip.

Blaring sirens echoed from every direction. Ben didn't move. He sat there, his heart feeling cold and lifeless within him, the chaos and activity around him a distant muffle.

More than one life had been devastated by the crash. Ben's own sense of assurance lay shattered.

———∞∞∞———

Peter set his keys on the kitchen counter, hungry for lunch after a busy morning of deliveries. As he headed for the fridge, his cell phone rang. He took it out of his pocket and looked at the Caller ID. It was Ben.

Peter answered it. "Hey, Ben! What's up?"

"Peter! Do you have a few minutes?" Ben's voice was strained.

"Sure. Is everything okay?"

"Something just happened that...that I don't think I'll ever forget." Ben's voice cracked and he had to pause for a few seconds. "There was an accident on the way home. A car accident. I saw the whole thing."

He told the entire story. He shared every detail. The car with the demonic symbol, the black SUV, the collision...the young man he pulled from the car.

"Peter, I am so shaken. My clothes are stained with blood. The police questioned me afterwards, and I just got home." He paused again, unable to stop the tears. Peter waited for him to go on.

"When I saw that man dying...when I heard his words and shared the gospel with him... something happened in my heart. I suddenly began to look at my own soul—and I wondered about my salvation." He took a deep breath.

"I know that God exists. Creation tells me that. I would be a fool to think that nothing created everything. What concerns me is that I don't really *know* that I am saved. I was telling a dying man that he could have assurance of everlasting life, and I don't know myself! I say all the right words and believe all the right things, but I'm having doubts, and it's driving me crazy. What happened today has brought it all to the surface. If that car hadn't been in front of me, it would have been me that took off at the green light...and I'd be the one who's dead. It's made me really think. You know what? I too would be terrified to die."

Peter took a moment to respond. "Ben...I don't know what to say. I'm so sorry..." He searched his mind for the right words. "I'll be praying for his family."

Peter drew a deep breath and prayed for wisdom. "Ben, I don't think you are alone with your doubts. It's very common. So I will give this my best shot and let you know how I deal with mine."

"Okay," Ben replied, eager for any reassurance.

"First, I just want to say that I know I'm a new believer—I've only been saved for about a year. But I've studied the Scriptures over and over on this subject, because I struggled with this too a few months back, and I just want to encourage you with what I've learned."

"Thanks, Peter. I'm listening."

"Okay. Here goes. The Bible tells us that we can *know* that we have eternal life. If there is anything in this life you and I should be sure all of, it's where we are going to spend eternity.

The Scriptures say, 'He who believes in the Son of God has the witness in himself.' That's 1 John 5:10. Is that what you're lacking?"

"I thought I had it, until today."

"Okay. Then let's go back to square one. The Bible tells us that when the gospel came, it came 'in much assurance.' So the fact that you want assurance is to be expected. And if you don't have it, there is a possibility that you've had a false conversion. The first step is to go slowly through the Ten Commandments and let their spiritual nature thoroughly search your heart. You know what that means?"

"Yeah. The Commandments bring 'the knowledge of sin.'"

"Right. That's their purpose—to act as a mirror so that we can see ourselves in truth. So let's do that now. How many lies have you told in your whole life? Think about the times you twisted the truth or deceived people, or dishonored your parents when you were a teenager by not being truthful about where you'd been. You don't need to answer out loud; just answer in your heart. And be brutally honest. Remember, God sees your secret sins.

"Now listen to what Jesus said about lust. He warned, 'Whoever looks at a woman to lust for her has already committed adultery with her in his heart.' Have you ever looked with lust? Have you stolen anything in your life, regardless of its value? Have you used God's name in vain? Think about the sin of using His holy name as a cuss word. Blasphemy is so serious. Ben, if you have done these things, our morally perfect Creator sees you as a lying thief, and a blaspheming adulterer at heart. If you are found guilty on Judgment Day, the Bible says you will justly end up in Hell."

Ben was quiet so Peter asked, "Are you still there?"

"Yeah," he sighed. "Yeah . . . I'm thinking that I've never seen how bad I am in God's eyes. You know something else? I don't think I've been fully submitted to the Lord. I've been going through the motions, but I want to do my own thing. I'd rather have praise and acceptance from the world than from God, so I've been hiding the fact that I'm a Christian when doing my comedy. And I've watched movies that I'm sure God would frown on—movies with blasphemy, among other things. I justified myself by accepting it as being cultural; it's just the way people talk. Not only that, but I've been compromising a bit lately. I've had sexual thoughts that I didn't dismiss too quickly, if you know what I mean."

"Yeah," Peter readily agreed. "I do know what you mean. Before I came to Christ I lived for lust. Loved it. It was my never-ending source of pleasure. But when I found out that in God's eyes I was committing adultery, it was like an arrow went through my heart. And that was just the Seventh Commandment. While we think that these are sins against other people, they are primarily crimes that we have committed against God Himself, because it's His Law that we've broken. Some are more obvious than others. We fail to keep the First Commandment by loving the One who gave us life with all of our heart, soul, mind, and strength. You're familiar with what King David did, aren't you?"

"Yeah. He committed adultery, and then killed the woman's husband because she was pregnant."

"That's right. He was trying to cover his sins. Then God sent Nathan the prophet to wake him up from his delusion."

Just then Ben butted in. "Hang on, Peter, I have an incoming call. It looks like it's the policeman I spoke to earlier. I gave him my number. Better take it. I'll get back to you, mate."

CHAPTER SIX

"Hello? Ben speaking."

"Mr. Price, it's Officer Miller. I just finished speaking with the mother of the victim, and she asked if she could speak with you. The poor woman is obviously very distressed. She said she'd really like to talk to you about what happened. I know it's unusual, but can I give you her number and leave it up to you about whether to call?"

Ben's chest tightened with grief. "Sure," he said after a pause. "I'd be happy to."

"Her name is Mrs. Sanford, and her number is 555-2587."

"Got it. I'll call her right away."

Ben hung up and took a deep breath. What in the world could she want to talk with him about? It was painful enough to think about what had happened, let alone tell the gory details to the boy's mother. This wasn't going to be easy. He tried to ignore the rapid thumping of his heart as he dialed the number.

The gentle voice of a woman answered the phone. "Hello?"

"Hello." He tried to keep his voice steady. "My name is Ben. The police asked me to give you a call."

"Oh, Ben, thank you so much for calling. It means a lot to me."

He could hear the strain in her voice.

"May I ask you what happened?" she inquired gently. "Did my son Corey, by any chance, say anything before he died?"

Ben related the entire incident, being careful not to talk about the masses of blood and the terror in Corey's eyes. As he hesitantly gave the details of the short conversation, he could hear Mrs. Sanford breathing deeply with emotion. It was less than an hour since she had heard of her son's death, and he couldn't imagine the intense pain she was enduring.

"I'm so sorry," Ben murmured, as he waited for her response.

"No, it's okay, Ben," the woman assured him. "These are not only tears of sadness, but tears of joy. Let me explain."

She took a deep breath and continued. "I'm a Christian . . . and this is going to sound a little strange, but every day for years I have prayed for my son Corey, that God would send someone to speak to him before he died. He was brought up in a Christian home, but he refused to go to church anymore after he became a teen, and he said he no longer believed the Bible was true.

"Recently I told Corey that I prayed for him daily—that God would send a Christian to speak to him before he died. He laughed when I said that, and made fun of me. He told me that he didn't believe there was 'a god,' and that there was no such thing as sin. You are my answer to prayer. I am overwhelmed by the fact that God sent you to speak to my son before he passed away. I can hardly believe that he has given his life to the Lord, and I am filled with unspeakable joy."

Deeply moved by what he was hearing, Ben managed to pray for her, that God would comfort her in her loss, then he hung up and broke down in tears. He felt he should pray for her in those circumstances, but in reality, he was the one in greater need of prayer.

———— ∞ ————

The phone seemed to ring a hundred times as Ben waited for Peter to answer. He was anxious to tell him about his phone call.

"Hey, Ben. Sorry about that. I started cooking something and it decided to overflow out of the pot into the flame. Gas stovetop."

"Yeah. Know what you're saying. Hey, that call was the policeman, asking me to phone the kid's mother. It looks like my being at the accident was an answer to prayer. She said she had prayed that someone would share the gospel with her son before he died. Man ... all this is tearing at my emotions. I'm humbled, shocked, worried about my own salvation ... and confused. I sure appreciate your friendship and your help."

Peter was thankful for Ben's honesty, and picked up where he had left off.

"You know what has helped me more than anything else in my Christian walk?" He didn't wait for an answer from Ben. "The fear of the Lord. I'm careful who I say that to because it's probably the most hated of the Christian beliefs. I made the mistake of telling my neighbor that I feared God, and did he go off on a rant! He went on and on about God being love and that we shouldn't do anything out of fear, and that people who go around telling others that they should fear God should be locked up. But Jesus said to fear God, and all you have to do is spend a few moments reading the Psalms or Proverbs and you'll see how important it is."

Ben piped in, "I think that's what I lack. I have this image of God that's kind of like a happy Santa."

"I know what you mean. It's an idol that needs to be replaced with the biblical revelation of what God is really like. You know the story of David and Bathsheba?"

"Yeah. I love that story."

"Right. Nathan the prophet shows up—after the king had committed adultery and murdered Bathsheba's husband—and he put the fear of God in him. It was the knowledge that David had sinned against God that produced in him the sorrow that he needed in his repentance. Listen to his words . . . hang on a minute . . . Here it is, Psalm 51:

Have mercy upon me, O God,
According to Your lovingkindness,

According to the multitude of Your tender
   mercies,
Blot out my transgressions.
Wash me thoroughly from my iniquity,
And cleanse me from my sin,
For I acknowledge my transgressions,
And my sin is always before me.
Against You, You only, have I sinned,
And done this evil in Your sight—
That You may be found just when You speak,
And blameless when You judge.

Ben was moved. "Wow. That sure pinpoints
my problem. I've never come to God with that
attitude."

"That brings us to step two. Make sure that
you believe God's promise of forgiveness through
the cross: 'If we confess our sins, He is faithful
and just to forgive us our sins and to cleanse us
from all unrighteousness' (1 John 1:9)."

"Yeah. Step two is the big one for me. I
think this has been my problem. I've always had
trouble with having faith in God," Ben admitted. "I'm not sure why that is. It may be that I

like to try to work things out rather than just have faith."

Peter paused for a few seconds. "You know, I've been thinking about what you just told me...about Corey dying in your arms this afternoon. I don't think I believe you."

"What do you mean you don't believe me?" Ben exclaimed incredulously, his voice coated with shock. "It happened! Do you think I just made that up? I'm not lying to you, Peter. There was an accident and this guy died in my arms! If you don't want to believe me, that's your problem..."

Peter could tell that Ben was a little upset. He didn't like doing this after what Ben had been through, but he felt it was important. "I have trouble having faith in you, Ben," he added.

Ben was flabbergasted. "Come on, Peter..."

"You're upset aren't you?" Peter cut in. "I can tell by your voice. Let me explain why you're upset. If I don't have faith in you, if I don't believe something you tell me, it means I think you're a liar. You're not worth trusting. Now listen carefully. If you, a mere man, are insulted by my lack of faith in you, how much more do you think that you insult a holy God when you have a lack of faith in Him?"

"Whoa!" Ben breathed in wonder. "I never thought of it like that. You're right."

"If you and I look at a promise of God and even think 'how can I be sure this is true?' we're greatly insulting God and calling Him a liar. I think you're right when you said this could be your problem. Listen to this verse from First John: 'He who believes in the Son of God has the witness in himself; he who does not believe God has made Him a liar, because he has not believed the testimony that God has given of His Son.' The Scriptures say not to depart from the living God through an 'evil heart of unbelief.' Any lack of belief in God's promises is called 'evil.'"

"So with my doubt, I have actually been adding to my sins."

"True. Never, ever, insult God by doubting His promises. When Jesus said, 'Have faith in God,' it wasn't a suggestion; it was a command. Trust is what makes any relationship work. Of course, I believe what happened to you today," Peter assured him. "I wouldn't jeopardize our friendship by doubting what you told me. If you don't get this, you will never get anywhere in your Christian walk. Hebrews 11 says, 'Without faith it is impossible to please Him.' If you want to please God, trust Him. Are you with me?"

"I sure am. I must have been nuts not to have seen this. It's so simple, and yet so profound. I sure appreciate you telling me this, Peter."

"I'm glad to hear that. Let's do a quick trust test. Here are two basic promises of God: 'The one who comes to Me I will by no means cast out,' and 'Whoever calls on the name of the LORD shall be saved.' Do you believe these promises, or do you think God is lying?"

Ben sounded confident as he answered Peter. "Yes! I believe those promises with all of my heart." He laughed. "You know what? It feels good to say I believe God! This is so simple. How could I have missed it?"

"I have one more step for you, if you're interested..."

"Please keep them coming! This is like water to a man dying of thirst!"

"Okay. Here's step three, another promise from God: 'He who has My commandments and keeps them, it is he who loves Me. And he who loves Me will be loved by My Father, and I will love him and manifest Myself to him.'"

"Yes. I'm familiar with that: John 14:21. I memorized it."

"Do you believe it?"

"Absolutely. I do now. I wouldn't insult God with my unbelief."

Peter laughed. "I'm happy to hear that. This verse tells us that the Creator of all things will reveal Himself to any human being who obeys the words of Jesus. He does this by sealing us with His Holy Spirit, making us new creatures with a new heart and new desires. He gives us a love for His Word, a love for the lost, a peace that passes all understanding, a joy that's unspeakable, a delight to do God's will, and an inner witness that we are His children. We therefore have everlasting life. If I want the reality of this verse in my life, I simply trust and obey, because as the famous hymn says, 'there is no other way.'

"As you know, we are saved by grace through faith. Nothing we do can earn eternal life. It's the gift of God. However, the genuineness of our conversion will be evidenced by an obedient heart. We will want to please God. So we repent of all sin, trust in Jesus alone for our salvation, read the Bible daily without fail, pray without ceasing, and here's a big one—share the gospel with a dying world. Evangelism is love in action, so if the love of God is in us, we should go out of our way to reach people who are heading for Hell.

"And this is something I'm just learning to do myself. I have to admit it is kind of scary to risk having people think I'm a narrow-minded, intolerant, religious nut—you know how it is—but I've really been feeling that if we love people, like God commands us to, we can't be silent about something so important. We have to warn people."

CHAPTER SEVEN

The afternoon sun sparkled bright and blazing against the deep blue hue of the sky. Peter, with Ben beside him in the passenger seat, directed his car through traffic, heading for the comedy club.

"You doing okay, Ben?" Peter asked his friend as he merged onto the freeway.

"Yes, I'm doing much better, thanks," Ben replied with a grateful smile. After their long talk that afternoon, Ben had been greatly encouraged. First, the fact that he had been an answer to Corey's mother's prayer was extraordinary to him. God had placed Ben in the right place at the right time. How patient He had been with Corey, and how patient He had been with Ben! Such thoughts inspired in Ben a great awe—and fear—of Almighty God. Ben was also confident that one day he would see Corey in heaven, and that made his heart soar with indescribable joy.

Still, he was too shaken by the accident to want to drive again so soon. So Ben asked Peter to come pick him up and go with him to the comedy club a couple of hours early. Ben wanted to have plenty of time to practice his new impersonations, and Peter could serve as his audience to give him feedback. Peter was delighted to spend his afternoon with Ben, enjoying his friend's comedy and cheering him on.

Peter grinned, satisfied at Ben's heightened spirits. He knew Ben would probably still struggle with memories of the accident, but he knew that God would give him peace and comfort as well. He had also been praying for Ben's Christian walk, that God would continue to help him grow stronger in his faith and overcome his doubts.

"Hey, how about we stop and grab a bite to eat?" Peter asked. His hurried lunch hadn't quite hit the spot.

"You can if you want. I'm not really hungry. Nerves, I guess." Then Ben added, "But we need to stop somewhere anyway and get a hammafor. I need one for tonight's routine."

Peter did a double take. "A what?"

"A hammafor. They're pretty hard to get nowadays. You don't know what it is?"

"Never heard of it."

"I can't believe you've never heard of a hammafor!"

Peter was incredulous. "What's a hammafor?"

"Banging in nails." Ben grinned. "Fell for that one, didn't ya?"

"Sure did!" Peter laughed. After a few moments he continued, "I've got to stop and get something to eat. I'm starving. I could eat a whole py-cost."

Ben looked a little mystified. "What's a py-cost? Ahhhh! I can't believe I just said that!"

———— ∞ ————

"What do you think, Sandra?" A young man flaunted the pair of sunglasses he was trying on, attempting to impress his girlfriend. "I think they make me look cool."

She rolled her eyes. "James, you're trying on sunglasses from a convenience store. Cool is not possible."

The couple were on their way to a friend's house for a barbecue. They'd been dating for about three months and Sandra was wondering how much longer the relationship was going to last. The fact that he wanted to stop and get some new shades just to look cool exemplified his shallow character. He could hardly walk past a mirror or a window reflection without stopping or at least slowing down to admire himself. Though some days she thought she loved him, other days—like today—she felt impatient with his over-inflated ego. He always seemed to be thinking of himself first.

As James continued to check out sunglasses, two young men entered the small shop and stood behind him, patiently waiting to look at the glasses.

James glanced over his shoulder and noticed them. "Do you guys need to get in here?"

"No, no hurry," one of them answered pleasantly as he shook his head.

"Are you two together, or do we have a line?" James added derisively.

"We're together," one man said, glancing at his companion with an affectionate smile. They appeared to be more than just friends.

James went back to his fashion show, not the least bit concerned that he was keeping the two men, and his girlfriend, waiting. He glanced up at Sandra to model the latest pair of shades when he noticed her worried look.

"What? You don't like these?"

Sandra leaned in, bringing her voice down to a whisper. "Don't stare, but there's a man over there who's acting suspiciously. I've been watching him pace back and forth. There's something really weird about him."

A few aisles over, a disheveled man with a shaggy beard and long, unkempt hair walked up and down the row, trying to look busy but not doing a very good job of it. He seemed anxious, as if he was waiting for something; his eyes darted nervously from side to side.

James typically shrugged it off. "Maybe he just needs some sunglasses," he joked.

Sandra sighed in frustration. "I'm serious. I think he may have stolen something."

Just then, a car pulled into a parking space in front of the store. A young man got out and walked around to the other side of the car. He leaned down to speak with the passenger through the open window.

"Sure you don't want anything?"

"No, I'm good," Ben said. "I don't usually eat before a gig—butterflies, you know."

"You eat butterflies? Yuck," Peter laughed. "Oh, I've got a joke for you, by the way. Knock, knock."

"Really?" Ben wrinkled his nose. "Okay. Who's there?"

"Interrupting starfish."

"Interrupting star—"

Suddenly Ben found Peter's palm on his nose and his fingers wrapped around his face.

"—uh!"

"Do you get it?" Peter said laughing.

"Yeah," Ben said. "I got it, right in the face."

Grinning, Peter left Ben and entered the store, heading for the snack area.

A few customers were milling around, and in the afternoon lull the cashier, a heavy-set man, filled the time by reading a paperback. Peter compared his options as he eyed the various snacks and candy items.

Suddenly, a yell shattered the quiet into a million pieces.

"Everybody get down. Get on the ground! *Now!*" the haggard, long-haired man screamed, swinging his outstretched arm in every direction, a gun in his hand.

A robber with a gun. That's all it took to activate an avalanche of horror in Peter's soul.

As everyone else immediately complied, Peter could only stand there, frozen in place by an overwhelming shock. It was as if he had been catapulted back fifteen years to a bank in the Midwest.

The robber turned his blazing eyes on Peter. He pivoted to point the weapon in Peter's direction, then with a roar of indignation, he ran at him.

Peter instinctively hit the ground. He didn't know how it happened, but adrenaline must have propelled him into obeying the criminal's orders. Several canned goods rolled across the ground beside him, knocked off the rack by his sudden movement. Sprawled flat against the cold, smooth floor, Peter cowered as the madman waved the pistol over his head.

"You want to be on the ground, or underneath it? Get down!"

He then rushed toward the cashier, waving his gun, and screamed, "Are those cameras on? Are they recording?"

The terrified attendant stammered, "No, no. I mean yes."

"No, yes—which one?"

"Yes, yes."

This only angered the gunman more.

———— ✧ ————

Sitting outside in the parked car, Ben was playing a game on his phone while he waited for his friend. A sudden shout and commotion jolted him out of his concentration, causing him to jerk in surprise. One quick glance through the store windows gave him a clear view of the situation.

Horrified, he automatically slid down in his seat, trying to keep out of sight in case the gunman spotted him and decided to prevent him from calling the police. Ben immediately dialed 911, his fingers clumsy and sweaty as he pressed the numbers.

After making a quick report of the situation, Ben hung up and pulled up Diana's number on his phone. He sent her a hurried text message: PETER IS IN TROUBLE. GUY HAS GUN. NOT JOKING. PRAY!

He wasn't sure about her religious beliefs, but he knew that most people pray, especially in a crisis—and this was a crisis. In his own heart, he cried out to God to keep Peter safe and deliver him from possible death.

───────── ∞ ─────────

Diana sat on her couch, her gaze transfixed on her laptop screen. Several hours had elapsed since she started watching clips on the Internet during her break that morning. It was now nearing dinner time and the first thing she did when she got home after noon was get back to the clips. They were addicting.

In the middle of one of the clips, Diana's cell phone buzzed, alerting her to an incoming text message. Pausing the video, Diana reached over and picked up her phone, discovering that the message was from Ben. As she read it, a look of dismay came over her face.

PETER IS IN TROUBLE. GUY HAS GUN. NOT JOKING. PRAY! The words pierced her heart like daggers.

Diana dropped the phone into her lap. Stunned, she sat for a moment, overwhelmed and uncertain of what to do. She glanced down at the message once more. The last word implored her: PRAY!

Pray? She couldn't remember the last time she had prayed. Should she pray in her mind? Would God hear her? Would praying even make a difference?

Diana drew a deep breath, attempting to keep her racing thoughts at bay. After several seconds, she closed her eyes, and said quietly, "God, if You can hear me . . . please protect Peter." Her heart tightened with fear as she prayed, and yet a faint hope flickered inside her.

From his position on the ground, Peter watched the robber choose the store clerk as his next victim. He rushed at the front counter, aiming his gun at the cashier's face. The man could only tremble as the criminal shouted at him in a demanding voice.

"Give me the cash! I need the cash, now!"

"Nobody pays with cash anymore," the clerk whimpered pathetically.

Momentarily dazed by this revelation, but unwilling to admit defeat, the robber growled in fury. Without skipping a beat, he spun around, and spotting a girl cowering on the floor, ran at her with his gun hand extended.

With the weapon just inches from the top of her head, he shouted at the clerk, "Open the safe, or I'll open her skull!" Sandra trembled in terror, holding her hand over her mouth, trying not to become hysterical.

Images from his memories seared through Peter's brain. Crazed eyes. A gun barrel. A terrified woman. He could barely believe that the most horrifying nightmare of his life was becoming a reality for the second time.

Remaining in his prostrate position would keep him out of harm's way, but as he watched the petrified girl cringing beneath the robber's gun, compassion drove him to do the unthinkable. Before Peter realized what he was doing, he found himself on his feet, and he heard his own voice shouting, "No, no, no. Don't shoot her! Please! If you kill her, . . . you'll have to answer to God."

"What?" the thief spat in disbelief. "Who are you, Mother Teresa? What, am I gonna go to Hell?" His whole demeanor screamed with mockery.

The two male customers were sprawled nearby, huddling together as the chaos unfolded. Suddenly, one of them, after watching the commotion over Sandra, spoke up in protest.

"Leave her alone, man! Please, just give me the gun..."

The criminal's lightning-fast reactions caught them all off-guard. He shoved his gun onto the back of the man's head and said, "Yeah? You want the gun? How about I give you my bullets instead!"

"Where are these two gonna go if I pull the trigger?" the thief taunted Peter, the gun hovering over both men's heads.

Peter's heart clenched at the question. The two men trembled beneath the gun as one of them grasped the other's hand.

"No, don't shoot!" Peter yelled in panic and desperation. "Look, if you're going to shoot anybody...shoot me."

As the gunman turned on him and barreled toward him with the weapon outstretched, it dawned on Peter that he had just pronounced his own death sentence.

The madman grabbed Peter roughly by the shoulder and pushed the muzzle of the gun against his forehead. The cold metal caused a tingling sensation to ripple across Peter's skin. The memory of another gun against his forehead was vivid in all its terror.

"Please, God," Peter murmured under his breath as he closed his eyes, "I don't want to die." Turning to his captor he screamed, "Look, just don't shoot anyone, okay!"

Aghh!" The robber shook with fury, yet couldn't seem to bring himself to pull the trigger.

And that's when blaring sirens could be heard.

As quickly as the criminal had seized Peter, he released him with a shove. Peter felt his knees go weak at being so close to death…again. Police sirens approached from every direction as the robber's anger boiled over.

"No, no, no. This isn't happening!" he

screamed, spinning about wildly with accusing eyes. "Who called 'em?"

He pointed the gun once again at the poor store clerk. "Did you call the cops?" he demanded.

The clerk held his hands out as if to stop an onslaught of bullets, saying, "No!" in the hope he would be believed.

Outside, the parking lot was now filled with police cars. The cops were ready for him.

Undaunted, the criminal went to his last resort. Finding Sandra still huddled on the floor, he growled, "Get up! Get up!" He grabbed a fistful of her shirt and hoisted her to her feet. With her firmly in his grasp, he dragged her out the door in front of him.

What he encountered outside was more intimidating than he anticipated. This was definitely not the way he'd planned it to go. Surrounding the store in a semicircle were several police cars, with officers positioned behind the open doors of the vehicles—their weapons aimed straight at the gunman.

"Put your weapon down!" one of the policemen demanded. He had his own gun leveled at the criminal, but with the girl in the way, he could only wait until his orders were obeyed. "Put it down now and you will not get hurt."

"Let her go!" the other cops hollered at him, but the thief only jeered at them.

"Get out of here!" he roared, pacing back and forth in front of the store, holding his pistol against Sandra's head as he dragged her with him. "Back off or I'll shoot her! She's gonna die, and it'll be all your fault!"

Inside the store, Peter slowly stood to his feet, his body alert. He felt lightheaded after his life-threatening experience, and as he listened to the commotion outside, all he wanted to do was get out of there.

The others in the store were partially hidden from his view as they stayed put, not daring to move. But suddenly, one of them jumped to his feet and bolted for the back exit. It was James showing his true colors. He didn't care about Sandra. All he cared about was his own pretty face. *Maybe I should get out of here too*, Peter thought. He could escape to safety without a scratch. All he had to do was make a run for it.

"Somebody help me!" A woman's desperate plea. The criminal's hostage.

Peter felt like his heart was being torn in two. He couldn't leave. Ever since that traumatic day as an eleven-year-old boy, he had been afraid, terrified of any circumstance that required boldness and courage. But he couldn't be a coward like James. If her own boyfriend wouldn't help her, then Peter would have to step up and save her himself. The police had repeatedly demanded that the robber drop the gun, but he just kept yelling that she was going to die. The man was desperate, and so many times these incidents tragically ended in bloodshed.

As the standoff continued outside, Peter looked around frantically for a solution. That's when he spotted the canned goods he had knocked over a few minutes earlier.

That was his answer. It was pathetic, but it was his only option.

Back outside, the police officers were nearing the end of their patience. The thief had threatened and yelled at them for too long. It was time for them to take action.

"Put your gun down and let her go. Put it down *now!*" the officer shouted one last time. But it was no use. The command once again fell on deaf ears.

Peter clutched a can in his right hand, his heart hammering in his chest as he strode boldly toward the front. A few feet ahead stood the crazed thief, pacing back and forth with Sandra firmly in his grasp, his gun to her head.

The chaotic situation gave Peter the opportunity to approach the man from behind without being noticed. Taking a deep breath, he pulled his arm back, calculated his aim, and hit the robber's head with all the might he had in him.

The man crumpled to the ground, releasing his grip on Sandra and giving her the chance she needed to run for it. Dazed and barely coherent, the defeated criminal lay sprawled on the cement as the officers descended upon him. "Grab the gun!" one of them shouted, and as soon as it was confiscated, they handcuffed him and dragged him to one of the squad cars.

Peter surveyed the scene in shock. He could barely believe what he had just done. At that moment, the other two customers walked out of the store, looking around in astonishment. One made a beeline for Peter and grabbed him in a huge bear hug of gratitude. Surprised, Peter patted his back in response, still trying to process everything.

From inside the parked car, Ben slowly raised himself up in his seat to see what had transpired while he had been hidden from view. After surveying the scene and finding that everything seemed to be fine, he let out a sigh of relief.

Diana heard her phone buzz, snatching at it like a thirsty man grabbing at a glass of water. With shaking hands, she read the text message from Ben: PETER IS FINE! ALL IS WELL. POLICE HAVE THE GUNMAN.

Diana exhaled, relaxing her taut muscles, nearly laughing with relief. Her phone buzzed again. Several pictures came through: shots of Peter and Ben posing next to the gunman—secured in the backseat of a police car—and the police officers. Diana chuckled at their goofy expressions. Those two were always cutting up, even in the midst of such drama.

Diana's racing heart had finally slowed to its normal rate. She felt strange, as if a calming peace had descended over her. She had a sense of gratitude, such relief and joy.

Could God have heard and answered her prayer? Was it her prayer that had contributed to saving Peter's life? She didn't know. But she knew that either way, it must have been God who had delivered Peter.

Closing her eyes once again, she whispered, "Thank you."

CHAPTER EIGHT

Peter shook hands with the police officers as he turned to go, reaching for the car keys in his pocket. Ben had been patiently waiting for him in the car.

"Excuse me…" Peter glanced up at the sound of a man's voice. He found to his surprise that the two men from the store were still there, waiting in the parking lot.

Peter gave them a friendly smile. "Hey. You guys doing okay?"

"Yes, thanks to you," one of them returned with sincere gratitude in his eyes. He held out his hand. "I'm Lance."

Peter grasped the offered hand and gave it a firm shake as he introduced himself.

"I'm Robert," the other added, also shaking hands with Peter.

"Done with the police report?" Lance asked.

"Yeah, just finished."

Robert ran his fingers through his hair and threw a glance at his partner. "Hey, you almost took a bullet for us in there. Can we at least buy you dinner? I mean, to just go our separate ways after all this . . . well, it just seems kinda weird."

Peter paused uncertainly, looking over at his parked car. "Thanks for the offer, but I can't. I need to take my buddy to his comedy show."

Lance nodded, looking down as if in deep thought. "Well, could you possibly drop him off and then join us for a quick bite?"

"Yeah, it would mean a lot to us," Robert said.

"Well, all that crime fighting *has* made me hungry," Peter grinned.

"Great!" Robert replied. "Do you know where Tino's Grill is? Just down the street?"

"Sure, that sounds good. I do have a bit of time," Peter looked down at his watch. "I can meet you guys there in about forty-five minutes."

"Okay, we'll see you there."

⎯⎯⎯∞⎯⎯⎯

As Peter entered the restaurant, he found Lance and Robert seated at the bar, and he went to join them.

"I still can't believe you did that," Robert said incredulously.

A waitress walked by at that moment. "Could I get an iced tea, please?" Peter called to her.

"Yes, of course," she replied with a smile, hurrying away.

"Why would you do that?" Lance asked.

"Because I like iced tea…"

Impressionist Ben Price awaits directions from Eddie Roman before he begins his standup routine.

Peter sits in the audience at the comedy club and enjoys Ben's routine. Phillip Comfort (Ray's brother) is seated in the background.

In this deleted scene, it was humorous when Peter (Travis Owens) bowed in prayer and Diana (Molly Ritter) asked if he had a headache. The script called for a burrito, but for some reason he was filmed giving thanks for a muffin, which seemed a little weird.

Producer/Director Eddie Roman describes an upcoming scene to Mark Spence (Producer and Script Supervisor).

Peter encounters two lesbians and wants to share a gospel tract with them—but his fears get the better of him.

Preparing to shoot the elevator scene with the mean man (Kurt Sinclair, who actually seemed like quite a nice guy in real life).

Diana tearfully tells Peter of her brother's cancer.

Peter does a unique "Knock, knock" joke on Ben that never fails to get a laugh from the audience.

The police cars arrive for the robbery sequence.

The police aim their guns at the would-be robber. Scenes like this are so much fun to shoot.

"You want my gun? How about I give you my bullets instead!" Brad Snow (our graphic artist/webmaster) came up with this line.

We were all impressed with Jason Tobias. His portrayal of the robber showed his experience (at acting).

Two members of our staff do a "selfie" during the scary robbery sequence.

The police who arrested the robber—made up of our staff and a few friends. (Sunglasses are a must in Southern California.)

Diana meets Peter at the comedy club.

"I've just heard it all before and I'm done listening. I will not deny my sexuality."

Diana drives past the lone hitchhiker (Mariano Mendoza) on a dark road.

The hitchhiker violently pounds on the window of Diana's car and terrifies her.

The comedy club host (Todd Friel) announces that the next act didn't show up.

Peter is finally victorious in overcoming his stage fright. His comedy debut is a success!

Robert and Lance chuckled, catching on to Peter's dry sense of humor.

"But seriously, you don't even know us, and yet you told that guy to shoot you instead of us!" Robert exclaimed in disbelief.

Lance nodded solemnly. "That took a lot of courage."

"Actually, I was terrified." Peter leaned forward, looking the men straight in the eyes. He wanted to be completely open and honest with both of them, and he hoped they would see that he truly cared. "But I'm a Christian, and I know where I'll go when I die."

A moment of silence followed as a look passed between Lance and Robert.

"You're a Christian," Lance repeated, his friendly demeanor cooling a bit. "You know we're gay, right?"

Peter nodded. "Yeah, I figured that when I saw you holding hands, just before the guy came at you with his gun."

"But don't most Christians pretty much hate gays?" Lance continued.

"No, that's not true," Peter tried to reassure them. "We don't hate anyone."

An awkward pause followed. Robert glanced at Lance who took a slow sip of his beer.

Just then the waitress came over to tell them that their table was ready. As the two men followed Peter, Robert exhaled deeply, mumbling to Lance, "Well, this is a first. I can't say we've ever taken a Christian to dinner before..."

After they were seated, Lance spoke up. "You know," he began, "I actually have questions about the Bible and what it says about being gay."

"Really? That's weird. I was just looking into that."

Lance gave Peter a critical stare. "Really? Why would you do that?"

"I had this crazy nightmare," Peter shared, trying to choose his words carefully. "It left me thinking that if I'm not true to what the Bible says about homosexuality, it's like not warning people about a faulty elevator before they step into it. So if I really love people, I have to say something. Love can't stay silent."

An uncomfortable atmosphere began to settle over the conversation.

"Okay, speaking of love...," Lance remarked, leaning forward with his hands spread out on the table. "If God is love, why is there so much suffering, and death? And if homosexuality is such an abomination, why does the Bible also use the word 'abomination' to describe eating shellfish?"

Peter nodded, turning the questions over in his mind. "Okay..."

"Oh, one more," Lance added. "How come the word 'homosexuality' wasn't even in the Bible until a few decades ago?"

Robert squirmed a little, looking uncomfortable at Lance's barrage of questions.

"Okay, one at a time." Peter prayed for the courage to talk to them in love without turning the conversation into an argument. "That's true," he agreed. "The word 'homosexuality' wasn't in there because it hadn't even been invented yet. That word wasn't coined until sometime around 1900. But the original Greek word that was used is the exact equivalent of the modern word 'homosexuality.'"

"I didn't know that," Robert admitted, looking to Lance.

"Okay. What about the shellfish?" Lance reminded him.

The waitress returned just then and set Peter's iced tea on the table. "It comes with a baked potato and glazed vegetables," she piped in, assuming he was asking her.

"Oh . . . no, we're not ready to order yet," Lance explained.

"Okay, no rush," the waitress said politely.

As Peter sipped his iced tea, he noticed Robert handing the waitress a folded piece of paper. "Can you give this to Tino, please?"

"Sure thing!" She slipped it into her black apron and bustled away.

Peter reached down and rummaged through his bag, pulling out some literature, including a booklet titled "God and Sexuality" and a couple different gospel tracts. One of them was called "Why Does God Allow Suffering?"

Spreading them on the table, Peter said, "Here's one of the things I was reading," pointing to the "God and Sexuality" booklet, "and here's something that explains why God allows suffering. I think you'll find these pretty helpful."

Robert picked up one of the tracts—what looked like a million dollar bill—and smiled. Lance leaned back in his chair, folding his arms across his chest, a scowl growing as Robert began reading the tract.

Clearing his throat, Lance put a hand on Robert's arm. "Um, you know what... I think we should go."

Robert's eyes widened in disbelief. "What?"

Lance pushed himself to his feet. "We really appreciate what you did, but we're done here," he said very firmly, looking Peter in the eyes.

A look of surprise crossed Robert's face. "What's wrong? He just gave us some Christian stuff. So what?"

Lance ignored the comment. "Let's go."

"I'm not going anywhere," Robert insisted quietly, appearing embarrassed. "What's your problem?"

"I'm not going to sit here and listen to this."

"He saved our lives!" Robert seemed indignant at Lance.

"I really didn't mean to offend you," Peter offered, attempting to salve the situation.

Lance turned on him, his voice hard and cold. "Yeah, I know. You and every other homophobe never mean to offend us. Yet you still tell us we're going to Hell unless we change. I've heard it all before, and I'm done listening."

"Don't do this. Please," Robert pleaded.

"I'm not going back into the closet and I won't deny my sexuality."

"Lance, stop! He didn't do anything!"

"Fine. Get converted. See if I care."

Turning his back on both of them, Lance stormed off, but stopped in his tracks. He spun on his heel and returned to the table, leaning close to Robert. With his finger pressed onto one of Peter's booklets, he slowly spit out, "Do not bring that into our home."

Then he was gone.

Peter and Robert sat in a silent moment of shock.

"I'm sorry. I really didn't mean to offend you guys," Peter sighed.

Lance shook his head and smiled. "No, you didn't do anything. I mean, after what you did for us today, you could pretty much say anything you want, and I wouldn't be offended."

"I can understand why he's mad. I do."

"But can you understand what it's like to be in our shoes?" Robert revealed no signs of anger. Upfront and honest, he just genuinely wanted Peter to understand him. "Do you really have any idea how much we have to deal with?"

"I know that this is complicated, and I don't want to come off as a know-it-all," Peter said sincerely. "But you saw what I was willing to do for you today, and there are plenty of other Christians who would do the same thing because they sincerely care about you."

"I don't doubt that about you, Peter." Deep gratitude flooded Robert's eyes.

"The bottom line is that I believe the Bible, and even though I'm terrified to do it, I have to speak the truth no matter what people think of me. Actually, it's not even about me. It's about this wonderful, loving God who sent His Son to die on the cross and rise from the dead, so that sinners could be forgiven and have everlasting life."

Footsteps approached the table, and the two men looked up to see that the waitress had returned. "Okay, what can I get for you guys?"

After they placed their orders, Peter reached over and picked up one of the tracts on the table. "You're doing a great job," he said, handing it to the waitress. "Here's a million dollars for you."

The waitress laughed good-naturedly, glancing at it as she walked off. "Now I can quit my job!" she commented over her shoulder.

Robert fingered another million dollar bill still lying on the table. "What is this exactly?"

Peter turned the tract over and pointed to a printed message on the back. "On this side of the tract is the gospel. When I hand these out to people, my main hope is for them to read it."

"Would you explain this to me?"

"Sure." Peter began to read it aloud, going over each sentence with Robert, explaining them in his own words after reading each one. He went through the moral Law, the Ten Commandments, emphasizing the importance of recognizing that everyone has sinned by breaking God's commandments. "My big revelation was that He saw my thought life," Peter confessed. "I didn't know that, and I was burning with lust, or what the Bible calls unlawful sexual desires. The truth is that all of us are in big trouble."

Peter then dove into the good news of the gospel, sharing that God made a way for everyone to go to Heaven—by Jesus, God's Son, coming to earth in the form of a man, dying on the cross to pay the penalty for the sins of the world, and rising from the dead. All one needed to do was repent of their sins and put their faith in Christ, and He would wash them clean of their sins and save them from eternity in Hell.

Robert soaked everything in like a sponge. His open heart and willingness to learn more spurred Peter on. He tried to make this biblical message as clear as he could, hoping with all his heart that Robert understood.

Peter paused as the waitress approached their table yet again. This time she brought something.

When she set it down on the table, Peter discovered it to be a slice of chocolate cake, with words written on the plate in chocolate syrup: "Thanks, Peter!"

Peter looked up at Robert in pleasant surprise.

"I wanted you to know how grateful I really am," Robert said. "I'll never forget what you did for us."

As they were finishing their conversation, Peter glanced up to see their waitress approaching with another waitress beside her. "Hey, can my friend get one of those too?" She pointed to the million dollar bills on the table.

"Of course!" Peter handed another one to her friend.

"Thank you so much!" Both waitresses grinned and walked away.

"Those are pretty cool," Robert admitted.

"Yeah, people love them. So, Robert, are you getting all of this? Does it make sense?"

Robert nodded, his eyebrows furrowed in a thoughtful way. "Yes, it really does."

"I am only telling you all of this because I truly care about you."

"I believe that."

———— ⬤⬤⬤ ————

Robert picked up the materials from the table and tucked them in his back pocket as they got up to leave the restaurant.

"Thank you for inviting me to dinner," Peter said warmly, as he and Robert stood outside, ready to part ways.

"It's the least I could do." Robert held his hand out, giving Peter a hearty handshake. "Thank you not only for saving my life, but for sharing all that with me. That took a lot of courage."

As the two men separated, both were thrown into a state of deep thought. This was a day they would never forget.

CHAPTER NINE

"I don't know how many people know the Simpsons," Ben said to the audience. "I've got the Homer Simpson GPS." Then he launched into a spot-on imitation of Homer's voice: "You'll be driving along the 71. We're going to take the next exit on the left. Wait, was it the left, or was it the right? Hang on, think. What are we gonna—*doh!* I dunno. Just stop here for some donuts. Mmm, donuts. Is there anything they can't do?"

Peter joined the crowd's hearty laughter, enjoying another night at the comedy club. Ben stood on the stage, beaming as the audience laughed with gusto at his impersonations. Peter could see the satisfied expression on his friend's face. He felt happy for him.

After several more impersonations Ben finished his act to a roar of applause, and the emcee took the stage.

"Come on, y'all. One more time, give it up, come on," the lanky host prompted.

The audience happily complied with more cheering.

"Please, he wasn't that funny," the emcee quipped. "All right, consider this a union gig. We're going to take a five-minute break. If you're a government worker, that's about an hour. Everybody else, five minutes. Go in back, get yourself an overpriced, watered-down drink. Five minutes, everybody."

While the crowd dispersed to indulge in the refreshments, Peter gave the comedy club a quick sweep of his gaze, wondering if Diana would show up late—or if she'd forgotten again.

He reached into his pocket and pulled out his cell phone, checking to see if she had sent him a text message. As he looked at his phone, the sound of a woman's heels clicking across the floor approached his table.

Glancing up, he encountered the smiling Diana herself. Peter stood to greet her, and she gave him a big hug, exclaiming, "I'm so glad you're okay!"

"Me too," Peter said with a laugh, taking a seat at the table. It had been a very long day. After such trauma, he felt worn and tired—but overwhelmingly thankful. "Crazy, huh?"

"I can't believe that happened to you." Diana sat across from him. A timid smile tugged at her mouth. "I, uh, I actually prayed."

"No, you didn't," Peter said, astonished and very pleased.

"Yeah, I did. I can't remember the last time I did that."

"Wow. Well...thank you very much." The fact that she had not only prayed, but had prayed for *him* was very humbling. He smiled gratefully.

"So..." Diana hesitated, yet she was eager to share what was on her mind. "I've been watching the videos that you showed me all afternoon..."

Another surprise. Peter didn't want to embarrass her by showing his astonishment, so he only nodded to encourage her on.

"And...I haven't told anyone this..." Diana lowered her voice with an uneasy smile. "But I'm getting a little nervous, because it's all starting to make...sense." She paused as if articulating her thoughts. "You know, the whole thing about Heaven and Hell."

"Right." Peter turned her words over in his mind, trying to form the appropriate response. Diana gave him her undivided attention, her eyes revealing a genuine interest.

"So," Peter began, slowly and carefully. "You understand the gospel—the main message of the Bible?"

"I think so. We're sinners...and Jesus can save us?"

"Right." Peter gently clarified her simple understanding of the gospel. "Well, Jesus came to die on the cross *for* sinners. So when you repent and turn away from sin, and you put your faith in Him, you're saved from the punishment you deserve."

"Hmm." Diana nodded, her eyebrows furrowed in thought. Before either of them could say more, Diana's cell phone rang. She picked up the phone and looked at the Caller ID. "Sorry, I need to take this," she told Peter apologetically. She stood to her feet as she answered the phone. "Hey, Katie. What's going on?" A concerned expression crossed her face as she walked toward the back of the room. "Yeah, sure. I'll come right over."

At that moment, the show started up again as everyone found their seats. The humorous emcee took the stage once more. "Welcome back, everybody. Again, I just want to thank you all for being here tonight. Can I tell ya? You're a much better crowd than last night.

That's all I'm saying. I don't want to insinuate that they weren't very bright, but if the joke didn't begin with 'Knock, knock,' it was a little rough."

As the audience laughed and the emcee continued to rattle on, Peter's phone buzzed. It was a text message from Diana: "Gotta go. Family emergency. I'll explain later."

———※———

Diana pulled out of the comedy club parking lot, preoccupied as she headed for her brother's house. His wife had called, sounding very distressed on the other end of the phone as she explained that Eric wasn't doing well, and she needed Diana to watch their kids while she took him to the hospital.

Diana drew in a deep breath, trying to blink away her stinging tears. So many thoughts and emotions plagued her at that moment. It seemed as if all the walls she had built around herself, trying to blot out the pain in her life, came crashing down upon her.

An image from the past flashed through her

mind in vivid color. She was eight years old, hiding upstairs beneath the covers of her bed, cringing at the sounds that came from the first floor below. Screaming and violent shouting. It had been going on for almost an hour. The arguing had started a while back, but it seemed to worsen every day. Hearing her parents treat each other with such hatred and animosity brought her great fear. That night was just the first of many.

Diana's heart throbbed with deep hurt as she relived those moments and thought back to the years of struggle and pain. The divorce that followed her parents' crumbling marriage had shattered Diana's world.

Throughout her life she harbored resentment deep inside, until it became a towering mass that threatened to topple over. She had often questioned God, asking Him, "Why?" For Diana, there was never a question of whether or not He existed. What she couldn't understand was why He did nothing in the face of evil. The abuse from her father, the nights crying herself to sleep, the feeling of being neglected and abandoned by her own family. She had never understood it all.

And now her brother had cancer. Her best friend while growing up, and her closest family member, suffering—literally dying before her eyes. What would come next?

But as Diana drove her car through the dark, almost empty streets, everything she had heard in the videos resurfaced in her thoughts. Her whole world was being shaken to its core. What astonished her the most was discovering that she wasn't a good person. All her life she had compared herself to others. She had comforted herself with the thought that she wasn't like her parents; she was a nice person, tolerant of everyone and kind to most people. She worked hard and assisted her elderly neighbor every week. She went to church a few times a year, paid her bills on time, never broke the law, and was always there for her family and friends.

But that's when she had been confronted with God's moral Law.

Several questions echoed in her mind, direct and personal ones that bared her soul. "How many lies have you told? Have you ever stolen anything? Have you used God's name in vain? Have you committed adultery in your heart by lusting?"

Those were just a few of the Ten Commandments. And Diana had broken each one of them.

She had never thought of lying and stealing as being major sins. But after watching the videos and opening her own Bible to search for the answers to her questions, she had discovered that even if she broke just one of God's commandments, she was guilty of them all. Committing just one sin made her a sinner.

And sinners went to Hell.

Diana tried to block the thought of Hell out of her mind. She hated the reality of death and what came after it.

But now she knew another truth—something that went hand in hand with the terror of sin and judgment.

Something that claimed to carry hope. The death of Jesus on the cross, and His resurrection. Through repentance and faith in Jesus Christ, one could escape the terrible punishment of

Hell and receive salvation and everlasting life because of His sacrifice. This message promised a fresh beginning: Christ could wash away the blackened mess of sin and create a new being. Then, following this transformation, one could have a personal relationship with the Creator and look forward to eternity with Him in Heaven.

It sounds too good to be true, Diana thought. Something inside her couldn't fully believe this message, this incredible offer of hope and forgiveness.

Diana shoved the overwhelming thoughts out of her mind. She had to focus on getting to Eric's house in time.

Turning right at an intersection, she found herself on a narrow, two-lane road heading out of town. Thick fog had begun to creep in, and Diana couldn't suppress a nervous sensation in the pit of her stomach.

After about a mile, Diana spotted something —or someone—a few hundred yards ahead. As she approached, she realized it was a rather burly, Hispanic-looking man. *Why would he be walking out here alone at night?* Diana wondered, suspicious that he was up to no good. He spotted Diana's car and raised his hand in the air, his thumb pointing upward. A hitchhiker.

One look at his shaved head, bulky frame, and unpleasant, scowling face gave Diana every reason to keep driving and ignore the request. She looked away to avoid eye contact, and tried to pretend that he wasn't upset at her refusal.

With a deep breath, she shook off her anxieties and plunged into the fog.

<hr>

After another minute of banter with the audience, the emcee reluctantly made his announcement. "I would like to introduce our next act ... but apparently he's about as punctual as Axl Rose." He paused as blank faces stared at him in confusion. "We don't have a next act, that's what I'm trying to tell you."

From where Peter sat, he could see the emcee cringe as the audience tried to process the disappointing news. When there wasn't an immediate response, the host added, "And I'm really not even kidding. We, uh, don't have a next act."

Murmurs rippled through the audience. Complaints of disappointment emerged from various corners of the room. "I want my money back!" a bold fellow dared to holler.

But the host wasn't finished. "Now, here's the deal. You can all get really mad and start throwing stuff at me, or we can keep this party going, because we're like the NSA—I happen to know that there are some people in this crowd tonight who are actually funny. In fact, the whole night you've been looking up here and thinking, 'I could be funnier than *that* guy.'"

Peter chuckled, and deep down he felt a tugging to respond to the invitation. Yet he didn't know whether any confidence would kick in to help him put that urge into action.

—◦◦◦—

As the fog thickened, Diana felt as if she were entering a tunnel, with gray walls closing in on her from both sides. It almost seemed ridiculous to keep driving with the poor visibility, but she thought she could manage and make it to her brother's house. She had to get there. Eric had always been there for her, and she had to be there for him. His young kids were there alone.

After several minutes, Diana thought she felt a slight difference in the way her car was running. Hoping it was just her imagination, she ignored it and drive on. But when the vehicle began to shudder and lose speed, she knew something was wrong. Suddenly, her car stopped altogether, and she came to a complete halt.

Sighing in frustration, she eyed her gas gauge and discovered to her dismay that the needle was on Empty. *Great.* She could've slapped herself. In her rush to get to her brother's, she hadn't checked to be sure she would have enough gas to make it.

With no gas station nearby, she picked up her phone and made a call. A couple minutes later, she was informed that a tow truck was on its way and would arrive shortly. With nothing to do but sit and wait, she hung up and took a long, deep breath. Clenching the steering wheel, she tried to calm her racing heart. No matter how hard she tried, she couldn't suppress the uneasiness in the pit of her stomach. As she sat

in her car, defenseless in the middle of no-
where, all alone in the inky darkness and swirling fog, she felt helpless. Checking to be sure
her doors were locked, she still couldn't help
feeling a little scared sitting in the darkness.

———❧———

"So here is your chance." The host pointed his
index finger at the crowd and swept a challenging gaze over the audience. "Where are our wise
guys? And just in case you need to be bribed,
the food here is almost better than airplane
food, and we'll feed you and your table if you're
willing to come up here. So, where is our first
funnyman?"

Peter glanced around him, trying to detect
any signs of interest from anyone who would
be willing to answer the host's call. When whis-
pers and murmurs proved to be the only response, Peter's heart beat hard against his ribs.

———❧———

Diana tried not to look at the darkness and fog
outside her window. It only increased her anxiety.

Her former thoughts returned, nudging her, pricking her conscience. She hated the sinking sensation of guilt in her stomach. She felt so uncomfortable, so, so...

Dirty.

Why can't I just forget about all of this? she thought, angry and bewildered.

But she couldn't forget. She could not fight against it, couldn't push it out of her mind.

Desperate and overwhelmed, she picked up her cell phone and found herself dialing Peter's number.

With her phone to her ear, she listened to each buzzing sound as the device rang. Finally, the ringing stopped, going straight to voice-mail. Instead of hanging up, Diana took a deep breath, and when she heard the familiar beep, she began to leave him a voice recording.

"Hey, Peter, it's Diana." She groped in her mind for the right words, for the perfect way to present a smooth and un-awkward message. "Sorry I had to go earlier. I just wanted to let you know that I've really been thinking about everything we've been talking about. And...

I've even been feeling bad about my...*sin*." She laughed, trying to picture his surprise at her confession. "Yeah, I said the word 'sin'..."

As if glued to his seat, Peter couldn't force himself to stand up and break the ice. With all his heart, he wanted to get up on that stage. He loved making others laugh. Ben's urgings returned to his mind, intensifying his inner turmoil.

Beyond his desire to perform for others, he desperately wanted to conquer his fear. Nothing humiliated him more than the anxiety and panic that enveloped him every time he encountered a situation that required him to step out of his comfort zone.

As a child, he never suffered from this problem. He almost welcomed the chance to show off his boldness and courage.

Then, at eleven years old, that one fateful day, a traumatic event had ripped the bravery out of him, leaving him a defenseless coward.

Thinking back to a few hours earlier, it dawned on Peter that this day had been different. He tried to recollect what had spurred him into conquering his fear at the convenience store.

It had been a life-or-death situation. Lives had been at stake. His concern and love for those people had forced him into ignoring his fear and taking action.

It had been the same with Robert and Lance. Because of his love for them and his concern for their souls, he had overcome his fear and shared the truth of the gospel with them.

If he could do that, he could surely do something as simple as getting onto a stage and doing a few impersonations. The more he challenged himself and tried to ignore his feelings and take action, the easier conquering fear would become.

Perhaps, with God's strength, he would get past this lifelong struggle.

With a deep and shaky breath, Peter stood to his feet. With purposeful steps, he strode toward the stage before he could change his mind.

Blinking against the brightness of the spotlights, he tried to ignore the fact that hundreds of people sat before him, faces brimming with curiosity and expectation. Fumbling with his pockets and forcing himself to make eye contact with the audience, he managed to stutter into the mic, "Hey… there's a lot of you here tonight. Umm, do you guys like impersonations?"

When the crowd responded with a resounding *yes*, Peter geared himself up for his first impression, his confidence boosting up just a notch.

"Okay. Well… this is Russell Crowe." He paused for effect, and then…

"ARE YOU NOT ENTERTAINED?!" he roared, throwing his arms up in the air as if he were Maximus himself, standing in middle of the stadium, a victorious gladiator.

The crowd exploded with laughter and applause at the convincing impersonation and thrilling display. The pleasure and shock on their faces were enough to make Peter's heart soar.

"And if you're not entertained," he added in the same English accent, a smug look on his face, "I'll throw a phone at your face."

Another hearty roar from the crowd. They loved him.

CHAPTER TEN

—⚬⚬⚬—

The silence became too much for Diana to bear. With nothing to do but wait, she sat there, unable to rid herself of the overwhelming loneliness and increasing feeling of fear. Finally, she resorted to flicking on the radio, tuning into her favorite station. Blaring the catchy country music, she tried to drown out her swirling thoughts and emotions, hoping she would feel calmer with the upbeat music filling her car. Finding even that annoying, she turned it off and went back to her thoughts.

After several minutes, her frayed nerves began to relax. She reached for her phone to check the time.

That's when a shadow darkened her window.

A loud thump resounded through the car, making it quiver with the impact. Diana shrieked, her head whipping around toward the direction of the sound.

As if hit with a bullet, Diana jerked in terror. Flanked by fog and the backdrop of faint moonlight, an intense, scowling face appeared at the window. Diana stared at him in horror, recognition flooding over her.

The hitchhiker.

He slammed his hand against the window, shouting in Spanish, determined to get into the car. He wrenched on the locked door, continuing to yell something incomprehensible to Diana. *"Abre la puerta! Abre la puerta!"*

"Help!" Diana snatched at her phone, her only lifeline, and tried with trembling fingers to call 911.

Suddenly, the man disappeared from the window and out of sight. Diana lost hold of her phone, and it fell out of her grasp and in between the seats. She tried to retrieve it, fumbling with cold, shaking fingers.

And then the face reappeared.

This time, Diana didn't hold anything in. An ear-splitting, heart-stopping scream escaped her.

When the man shouted one last time, pulled his arm back, and shattered the window with a rock, Diana knew her doom was sealed.

The burly man unlocked the door, threw himself into the car, and grasped her arms in an iron grip.

"*Help me!*" Diana shouted, her voice a strangled, helpless cry.

The hitchhiker's grip only tightened, and though she kicked and fought and clawed and used every ounce of strength she possessed to resist him, he dragged her through the door with relentless determination.

She was halfway out of the car when a thunderous noise shook the ground and a roaring whistle pierced the air. As she was yanked forward, a blazing light blinded her and numbed her senses. A split second later, a gut-wrenching crash exploded into the night, and her whole world was thrown into a black nothingness.

Peter, following the landlord, climbed up the steps to the front porch, his heart heavy within him. As the older gentleman began to unlock the door of the apartment, Peter said, "I really appreciate this."

The landlord nodded. "I heard about the accident and want to help in any way I can."

Peter entered Diana's apartment. Everything was clean and in order. He examined the spotless home, hoping to find what he had come for. The empty silence made the place feel lonely and unsettling.

"I'll take a look upstairs," Peter told the landlord, and then headed for the staircase. When he reached the second floor, he came upon a small, open sitting area, complete with a cozy couch, a coffee table, and a bookcase, surrounded by homey decor. As he entered and examined the room, something caught his eye.

When he moved closer to the coffee table to have a better look, he was satisfied with what he saw. Lying open on the table was a large Bible— just what he had come to retrieve. Peter opened his mouth to call down to the landlord and inform him of his findings, when something stopped him.

A bright yellow streak on the page of the Bible caught his attention. Sitting down on the sofa, he leaned forward to scrutinize the open book. Peter discovered that Diana had highlighted a specific passage. He scanned the page, and his eyes widened at what he found.

The Bible was opened up to 1 Corinthians 6, and she had highlighted portions of verses 9 through 11: "Do you not know that the unrighteous will not inherit the kingdom of God?" Two more words were highlighted as well as underlined with black pen: "nor homosexuals."

Just below, she had circled and highlighted one last phrase: "And such were some of you."

Peter let it all sink in. He stared down at the carefully underlined words in wonder. He knew she must have been thinking through the subject of homosexuality, but he wondered why she had so specifically underlined those phrases.

Glancing up at the coffee table in front of him, he nearly choked. He could only stare, his mouth dropping wide open.

Two picture frames decorated the table, facing him in clear, vivid color.

In the frame on the left, carved into the shiny metal in elegant script, it read "Forever in love."

The frame contained a picture of Diana. But she wasn't alone.

She was with another woman.

Peter's gut twisted within him as he gawked at the picture of the two women with their foreheads pressed together in an intimate pose. The names "Diana and Hailey" were inscribed along the bottom of the frame.

In the second frame reality hit home: it displayed Diana and Hailey with their arms thrown around each other in a tight embrace.

Almost trembling, Peter removed the Bible from the table, closed it, and made his way to the staircase. He stopped at the top, his mind in tumult. After a moment he went downstairs. "I found it."

The landlord met Peter at the bottom of the stairs. "Great. Ready to go?"

"Yes, sir." Peter tucked the Bible under his arm.

Peter thanked the man and the two parted ways at the front door.

———— ∞ ————

About an hour prior, Peter had been relaxing at home, feeling good about his successful, but brief, comedy debut. Flipping through the TV channels, suddenly Peter stopped on a news item that widened his eyes. It looked like what was left of Diana's car! He could tell it was hers by a bumper sticker that said "If you can read this, you're tailgating."

He sat mesmerized as he listened to how a young woman had been rescued from her vehicle seconds before it had been hit by an oncoming train. Swallowing his panic, he called the news station to find out if they knew which hospital she'd been taken to.

As he rushed to the hospital, Peter prayed for her healing and survival. He stopped at the nurse's station to find out her room number and how she was doing.

"Well…" The nurse glanced down at her clipboard. "Diana is semi-conscious, but a nurse heard her ask for her Bible to be brought to her. As a Christian, I know how important that is."

Although surprised at the request, Peter offered to assist in finding Diana's Bible and bringing it to her. His already rising hope continued to steadily ascend. On top of her remark that the gospel had begun to make sense, this seemed to be another step in the right direction. He could only hope that she would live long enough to come to Christ.

Now, with the Bible in his possession, Peter climbed into his car and started the engine. But before driving off, he sat there for a moment, perplexed.

Diana? *A lesbian?*

He didn't understand how she had kept it such a secret. His mind reeled as the reality of the situation sank in.

He didn't feel angry. He wasn't disgusted or disappointed. He didn't feel superior to her or look down on her for being homosexual.

He was just...shocked.

He never would have guessed this to be the case. Although he had seen Diana and Hailey talking at work, he figured they were just friends.

Sighing in his confusion, Peter checked his cell phone out of habit. Suddenly, he remembered that Diana had left him a voicemail after she had left the comedy club. He was so distracted after the show that he had forgotten to listen to it.

Finding the message, he began to play it.

"Hey, Peter, it's Diana. Sorry I had to go earlier. I just wanted to let you know that I've really been thinking about everything we've been talking about. And...I've even been feeling bad about my...*sin*." She broke off into a self-conscious laugh. "Yeah, I said the word 'sin.' Anyway, I've actually been reading the Bible...and it's really making me think. But I'm not quite there yet. I definitely have some questions. As I've been reading, I've noticed that God often gives people second chances. And I like that, because...I could use a second chance. So, I just wanted to say thanks. I know I've been arguing with you about God and stuff, but you've been nice enough to put up with me." She paused, her voice coated with emotion. "So, I just wanted to say thank you for not giving up on me." He could hear the tears in her voice. "You're a true friend."

Peter was grateful that he'd been able to share the good news of the gospel with Diana. Now, would she repent of her sins and place her trust in Jesus Christ?

Maybe, just maybe, the train crash had happened in order to bring Diana one step closer to surrendering her life to the Lord.

But in order for her to become a follower of Christ, she had to survive.

Heavenly Father, Peter prayed as he pulled

into the street, his heart clenching within him at the thought of Diana losing her life. *Please save Diana. And not just her body, Lord, but her soul.*

—◦◦◦—

The ticking of the clock grew louder as Peter stared at the closed door, a bouquet of flowers in his left hand and Diana's Bible in his right. Without a soul in sight, Peter waited in the empty hospital hallway, his heart thumping against his ribs.

Just a moment beforehand, he'd been instructed by a nurse to wait outside the room while she checked Diana's vitals. It felt as if hours had transpired since then.

Finally, the door swung open. The nurse poked her head into the hallway, whispering, "You may come in. But just keep in mind that she's still a little groggy."

Peter nodded his thanks as she stepped aside for him to enter.

Peter quietly surveyed the still form of Diana on the bed. Her arm, wrapped in a cast, lay across her chest. Her breathing was soft and peaceful, as if she had fallen into a deep slumber. It was so fortunate that her injuries were relatively minor, compared to what could have happened. When the train plowed into the car, both Diana and her rescuer were hurtled through the air and landed violently on the ground, and she had a concussion from a severe blow to the back of her head. The doctors had her medicated and wanted to keep her under observation for a day or so, to make sure the swelling went down.

Greatly relieved to learn that Diana would survive, Peter stood for a few moments, then decided to leave. He turned to see where he could put the flowers...when something caught his eye.

Diana, he was pretty sure, had begun to stir. Her head moved ever so slightly, and her eyelids seemed to twitch as she began to regain consciousness. Peter held his breath.

———◦◦◦———

Quivering shadows. Blackened fog. Distant, muffled voices.

Nothing made sense.

Claustrophobic, suffocated, and utterly lost, Diana attempted to break free.

To escape.

She ran. Her feet felt nothing beneath them. She flew through time and space, ripping her way through spidery fog as she careened into the blackness beyond.

Then, all at once, she came to a bone-jarring halt. With her wanderings postponed, she tried to gaze ahead of her. An eerie silence hung in the atmosphere like a thick, stifling blanket.

Looking down, she discovered train tracks cutting across her path and into the terrain to the east. After several moments of staring at them in dull confusion, a banging sound caused her to jerk her head up in surprise. Just a few yards away, to her left, a parked car lay across the train tracks. Squinting, Diana found—with the help of the faint moonlight—that someone sat inside.

Panicked, Diana struggled to run in the direction of the car, hoping to help in some way.

But someone had made it there first.

Now much closer to the vehicle, Diana saw another individual. A man stood outside the car, banging on the window of the passenger's side, shouting and pleading in words she couldn't understand. There was no response from inside the car.

Suddenly, the ground began to tremble as a thunderous noise roared into the night. A train's piercing whistle followed; then a frightening, spine-chilling shriek.

Diana didn't want to look up, didn't want to see the metallic monster chugging down the tracks. A loud smash came from the direction of the car. Diana turned just in time to see glass shatter.

Throwing aside a large rock, the burly man opened the door and dove into the car, pulling out a young woman who fought and kicked against him, completely unwilling to get out of the vehicle and allow him to rescue her.

Diana's mouth dropped open in horror. *What was wrong with her?* He was saving her from certain death.

As the woman twisted and thrashed in the man's grip, Diana caught a glimpse of her face.

The young woman was herself.

Suddenly, a blazing light blinded her as the distant thundering became an ear-splitting roar. Diana turned her face away and plugged her ears against the sound of metal meeting metal in an earth-shattering crash.

All sense of sight and sound abandoned her. Thrown back into the same state of wandering and confusion, Diana tried to pry through the fog and her blurred surroundings. A thought invaded her subconscious.

I thought that man was trying to harm me. But because of my distrust of him, I didn't realize that he was trying to warn me and save me from sure death.

A sudden flow of gratitude washed away her inner fear and bewilderment.

All at once, the swaying shadows melted into a faint, gray light. The thick silence gave way to the gentle sounds of footsteps and lowered voices.

And then, as if plunging to the surface of a lake, Diana broke into consciousness. Her eyelids fluttered open, and gazing above, she blinked several times at the ceiling. Once the fogginess cleared, she lowered her gaze and stared straight ahead.

A man stood before her. Timid and uncertain, he held tightly to a bouquet of flowers, searching her face in deep concern.

An overwhelming warmth flooded Diana's heart. Peter. Just the sight of him brought hope to her soul. Perhaps he could help her through the tangled mess of her life. Perhaps he could bring her deeper into the Bible. Perhaps he could answer the millions of questions that she had been too afraid to ask before.

As with the hitchhiker, Diana had resisted people like Peter, thinking they were out to be hateful and harm her with their words. But now everything came into focus as she realized that they were just warning her of the danger to come.

She now saw her homosexuality as being sinful and against God's design. She felt ashamed and uncertain of how to relay these hidden secrets to Peter.

But with one look at the love and concern in Peter's face, she knew that he would understand. She knew that he cared for her. She knew that he could help.

Breathing a sigh of relief, she lifted her head, looked Peter straight in the eyes, and smiled.

APPENDIX

An Interview with Ray Comfort
About "Audacity"

With homosexuality being such a hot-button topic, why would you want to make a movie about it?

I didn't want to make this. After we made films about abortion and evolution, people kept asking for one that addressed the issue of homosexuality—because most Christians were very uncomfortable about how to deal with it and not sound hateful. But I insisted that it wasn't going to happen. Anyone who spoke against homosexuality was instantly vilified as though he were a hate-filled racist. Nobody wants that.

However, around April 2014, I was with a friend in Huntington Beach, California, when I saw two girls walking toward us kissing. I asked if they would like to be on camera, and to my surprise they said that they would. These two ladies gave me an amazing 14-minute interview about gay marriage, the morality of homosexuality, and the gospel . . . and they ended up thanking me for not being judgmental. Yet I hadn't compromised the gospel even slightly. It was as though God had dropped the foundation for a movie into my lap.

That night I wrote a script and sent it to Mark Spence (the main editor and producer of "180"). He wrote back, "Wow, wow, wow!!!!" I quickly called a meeting, and just over a year later, we have what we believe is a very timely movie.

How would you answer the popular question, "Are homosexuals born that way?"

We major on that question in "Audacity." Most pro-gay people are adamant that they are born that way, but I asked them two questions that gave them another perspective on the issue, and they immediately changed their minds. It's wonderful to watch.

While most of the film is scripted using professional actors, these live interview portions are not. It was a risk to include them, but they flow with the story and are very powerful. MovieGuide said, "The movie insists that these interviews are completely unscripted and real. If so, they are incredible."

We had prescreenings and asked a thousand Christians from different demographics for feedback. I told them that I took photos of our kids seconds after they were born and thought they looked beautiful. In retrospect, they looked more like ET. But love is blind.

I then asked them to tell us if our "baby" was ugly—before we showed the picture to the public. The feedback we received was invaluable. They said we needed character development. So we filmed three new scenes. But most of all they said they wanted to see street interviews. So we added more real-life witnessing clips. We were nervous about putting these into a scripted film, but it sure worked out well. It's seeing people change their minds about such a contentious issue that is so unique, powerful, and fascinating.

How would you respond to critics who say you're intolerant?

There's a lot of concern among Christians because we are being unjustly labeled as hateful bigots, on a par with racists, simply because we say that homosexuality is morally wrong. But we have no choice. The Bible is very clear that adultery is wrong, fornication is wrong, and lying and stealing are wrong. The Scriptures put homosexuality in a category with those sins.

Someone cynically wrote to me recently and said that there is no way any Christian can believe the Bible and not be hateful. Well, I can't wait for him to see the movie. It's going to stop his skeptical mouth. There is a way to do it, and I believe that we (by the grace of God) did it in "Audacity."

We had a special prescreening in Southern California for donors. I invited a hard-core atheist friend and his girlfriend to attend, and when they came up to me afterwards I wasn't sure how they would react. What Mike said was so positive I asked if he would put it in writing and give me permission to use it to promote the movie. He did. This is what he said: "Unlike most Christian films it is far from cheesy, and has a great, well-acted script. Most of all it is not heavy-handed, showing the Christian position on homosexuality without being intimidating or angry. Well done!" —Michael S. Martin

What he witnessed was real love in action. There is no hate in this movie. Not an ounce.

Today, some major church denominations are changing their long-held position and becoming in favor of homosexuality. What makes you so sure it is indeed a sin when other respected pastors are saying it isn't?

My opinion is irrelevant. What matters is what God's Word says on the subject. This is another area covered in depth by "Audacity." The issue of homosexuality is putting a chasm between those who love God and those who don't. You cannot separate God from His Word.

But the movie goes even deeper in using an opening scene that shows that those who speak the truth in love, speak the truth because they are motivated by love.

If anything in the movie is controversial, it is the powerful sequence which shows that those Christian leaders who give homosexuals a pass into the Church don't love them in the slightest. They are actually their betrayers.

What are you hoping people will come away with after seeing this film?

There is such a need for direction for the Church as a whole. Someone put this comment on my Facebook page: "Please, please, please release 'Audacity' as soon as possible. Christians need to be equipped to handle the subject of homosexuality. I found an article on my Facebook newsfeed portraying Christians in an extremely negative way...I have faith in the film, that it will help awaken people."

We want Christians to be encouraged and equipped about what they can say, and if they find the issue too contentious, we hope they will share the movie and let it do the speaking for them.

We are expecting a good response, because this is a huge issue. Millions of Christians are asking important questions, and we address them head on. I believe that "Audacity" has the power to change this culture (through the gospel), and even bring healing between the Church and the LGBT community.

Do you think it will surpass "180" in the number of people it will reach?

We are delighted with the reviews so far, and by the fact that a major TV network viewed it and wants to air it to 190 countries.

When a reviewer (who didn't pull any punches) wanted a link for review purposes, I was a little nervous. This is because I knew that he really liked "180," and that was a high bar to reach. Millions have seen that movie and loved it. I also wondered if he would be upset that we went through Hollywood, and didn't stick with Christian actors.

A few hours after I sent him a link, he wrote back, "This is the best film you have made yet. Congratulations on a job well done."

The press materials say that "Audacity" will offer an "unexpected" look at homosexuality. Why unexpected?

Originally, I couldn't see how we could make a movie and break free from the stereotypical ex-homosexuals who are now happily married with children. That's nice. It's also a little boring, and it would be watched only by the choir.

For a movie on this topic to be appealing to the general public, we had to strive for a fast-moving storyline with production excellence. So, we went through Hollywood. We chose actors by merit rather than their Christian worldview, because we didn't want bad acting to sink the ship.

We pulled together a script that was extremely compelling, and one that had unexpected twists and turns. We even put humor into it. It may make you laugh, and it may even make you cry. This is nothing like you would expect from a Christian movie about the subject of homosexuality.

I think that even the LGBT community is going to be surprised because it's not what they're expecting. They are going to see that we didn't want to stereotype or vilify homosexuals.

I have known for many years that there is a wonderful biblical key to speaking with homosexuals, in a way that loves yet doesn't compromise. I just wasn't sure how to package that message in a way that wasn't boring, predictable, or stereotypical. It took over a year of hard work, but we finally have it in hand.

How will those who overwhelmingly support gay marriage feel about the film?

While there are some who have already made up their minds, we believe that the movie will give another perspective to most people who are open-minded. There is a delightful portion in the movie where you watch pro-gay people change their minds on camera about the issue of whether or not homosexuals are born that way. This is simply because they were given another perspective. So I think that there's going to be a lot of mind-changing going on after people have watched it.

When you decided to make the film did you have any idea that you'd be releasing it as the Supreme Court was ruling on gay marriage?

I think you mean, did the Supreme Court have any idea that they would be making a ruling on gay marriage when we would be releasing the movie. Actually, we were surprised, but we can't help but feel that this is divine timing and provision. We certainly hope it is.

We are not the only ones. Troy A. Miller, the President and CEO of the National Religious Broadcaster's Network, said, "This perfectly frames the issue facing our culture. Especially the questions many young adults are faced with concerning same-sex relationships. Every Christian needs to watch this!"

What impact do you believe the Court ruling will have on society?

Over the last few years we have seen a tsunami of cultural change regarding homosexual marriage. Most of us find it hard to believe how quickly it came. It caught us by surprise. The Supreme Court siding with gay marriage is just one more step toward the deep pit of moral decadence. It will bring more confusion about what's right and wrong. That's a slippery slope for any nation.

What do you think of gay marriage?

Along with countless others, I watched the royal wedding of Kate and Prince William. I listened closely as the minister defined marriage as symbolic of the relationship between Christ, as the Bridegroom, and His Church, the pure white virgin Bride. That's why the bride traditionally wears white in a wedding ceremony. It represents the cleansed and spotless Bride of Christ, the true Church, made up of all true believers.

With a sober and cultured English accent, the minister then led William and Kate through the traditional wedding vows:

> Dearly beloved, we are gathered here in the sight of God and in the face of this congregation to join together this man and this woman in Holy Matrimony, which is an honorable estate instituted of

God Himself signifying unto us the mystical union that is betwixt Christ and His Church...and therefore is not by any to be enterprised nor taken in hand unadvisedly, lightly, or wantonly, but reverently ...in the fear of God, duly considering the causes for which matrimony was ordained...Therefore, if any man can show any just cause why they may not lawfully be joined together, let him now speak or else hereafter forever hold his peace.

Marriage is not to be undertaken without serious consideration, and is so solemn the witnesses are told to speak up publicly if they can show any reason why the man and woman should not enter into this sacred covenant. No one should attempt to enter marriage unqualified—for instance, if one or both are already married, they are immediate relatives, or they are not one man and one woman.

Then the minister brought out the reason he was soberly saying these things:

I require and charge you both as you will answer at the dreadful Day of Judgment when the secrets of all hearts shall be disclosed, that if either of you know any impediment why you may not be lawfully joined together in matrimony, you do now confess it. For be you well assured that so many as are coupled together otherwise than God's Word does allow are not joined together by God, neither is their matrimony lawful.

If I was at a wedding where someone was trying to enter into a marriage covenant that I knew was unlawful, as his friend, I would have to speak or forever hold my peace. If he was attempting to marry a married woman, it would be unlawful. If he was trying to marry a man, this too is unlawful, because it's not the joining of one man and one woman as a symbol of Christ and His Church. It would merely be a legalized union between two men. Redefining this type of union as "marriage" would be like me declaring that my beige VW Beetle is a yellow Lamborghini. The two are nothing like each other. To believe otherwise is to deceive myself. Two men (or two women) is "otherwise than God's Word does allow," so they "are not joined together by God, neither is their matrimony lawful."

There's a good reason the following verses begin by warning us against deception:

> Do not be deceived. Neither fornicators, nor idolaters, nor adulterers, nor homosexuals, nor sodomites, nor thieves…will inherit the kingdom of God. (1 Corinthians 6:9,10)

But the situation for each of us is even worse than it sounds. According to Jesus, if we as much as look with lust, we commit adultery in our heart (see Matthew 5:27,28). Each of us is in big trouble on the dreadful Day of Judgment, when the secrets of all hearts shall be disclosed. According to the Bible, we're all heading for Hell if God gives us perfect justice.

Whether we are fornicators, idolaters (those who make up their own image of God), thieves, adulterers, or homosexuals, we each need to repent of our sins and trust only in Jesus—who took the punishment for guilty sinners on the cross, and rose again on the third day.

How did America become so pro-homosexual?

Prior to 1962, what was then called "sodomy" was a felony in every state of the U.S. punishable by a lengthy term of imprisonment and/or hard labor. In 1973 a public announcement movie was produced called "Boys Aware," warning youths to beware of homosexuals. Here is part of the commentary:

> What Jimmy didn't know is that Ralph was sick. A sickness that wasn't visible like smallpox but no less dangerous and contagious, a sickness of the mind. You see Ralph was a homosexual—a person who demands an intimate relationship with members of their own sex.

This was the general public perception of what was seen in those days as the dark crime of homosexuality. How is it that in one generation (in just forty years), what was illegal and viewed as a sexual perversion not only became legal, but was celebrated as being good and natural?

To understand what has happened, we need to ask the question why Hollywood is so pro-homosexual. By "Hollywood," I mean the powerful multi-trillion-dollar entertainment industry of music, magazines, books, news media, film, and television.

Hollywood attracts a certain type of individual. These are people who are often intelligent, confident, talented, physically attractive, colorful in personality, proud, and crave attention. They are ultra ego-driven. They want to be rich and famous and will prostitute themselves to fulfill their all-consuming ambitions.

They are not the average, humble church-going "God and Country" American. Consequently, they are not the sort of people who gravitate toward the humility of Christianity.

Instead, they are naturally godless in their worldview, hate the God of the Bible because He requires moral accountability, and go out of their way to mock and blaspheme His name, both on and off the screen.

So, we have the most powerful industry in the world with no moral absolutes. And whoever controls the media eventually controls the culture. Their voice is so powerful, even corporate America bows to their godless agenda.

Like a solid dam of restraint, Hollywood's Hays Code held back the moral decadence for thirty years. But when it was discarded in the 1960s, the result was the sixties sexual revolution. Since then there's been a bombardment of sexually explicit music, videos, movies, magazines, and television. Men kissed men on screen and women kissed women at high-profile music awards. And a generation infatuated by celebrity and ignorant of the history of homosexuality embraced the gay lifestyle as normal and good.

Actors who professed faith in Christ were blacklisted, and those who had the audacity to speak against homosexuality were vilified as though they were racist.

In the past, Hollywood has been out of step with Middle America. But their message of sinful pleasure has been both relentless and persuasive. They have the nation marching to their tune. And now a dam of moral decadence has burst upon the nation.

The only hope of her salvation is the gospel of Jesus Christ.

What should be the Christian attitude toward homosexuals and transsexuals?

I saw a horrible clip some time ago of an Arizona preacher telling his tiny congregation that he hoped and prayed that a certain high-profile transgender person would die and go to Hell.

What concerns me with things like this is that the media jump on it, and take the opportunity to paint all Christians with the same hateful brush.

He then tried to justify his righteous indignation by pointing to the Bible's imprecatory psalms. They are the psalms where David shows anger (and even a violent attitude) toward his enemies.

While there is some debate about why such an attitude is displayed in the prayers of David, I believe that he was simply venting his anger in prayer.

Perhaps he was called "a man after God's own heart" because in real life he showed amazing grace toward his enemies. This was because he had dealt with his flesh in prayer.

We should do the same in private prayer. We should vent our frustrations and any anger, love our enemies, do good to all men, and even honor them (see 1 Peter 2:17), as Scripture commands us to do.

May we never exalt ourselves to the place of God and judge who does or doesn't deserve damnation in Hell. Instead, we should consider the example of Jesus, and His amazing love and mercy toward those who nailed His hands and His feet to the cross. His prayer, "Father, forgive them, for they do not know what they do," is a high bar to reach, but one for which we must daily strive.

Anyone can hate. It takes godly character to show love.

See **www.AudacityMovie.com** to watch "Audacity" and find details on the Video Study, DVDs, tracts, and numerous related resources.

RESOURCES

If you have not yet placed your trust in Jesus Christ and would like additional information, please visit LivingWaters.com and check out the following helpful resources:

The Evidence Bible. Answers to over 200 questions, thousands of comments, and over 130 informative articles will help you better comprehend the Christian faith.

How to Know God Exists: Scientific Proof of God. Clear evidences for His existence will convince you that belief in God is reasonable and rational—a matter of fact and not faith.

Why Christianity? (DVD). If you have ever asked what happens after we die, if there is a Heaven, or how good we have to be to go there, this DVD will help you.

If you are a new believer, please read *Save Yourself Some Pain*, written just for you (available free online at LivingWaters.com, or as a booklet).

For Christians

Please visit our website where you can sign up for our free weekly e-newsletter. To learn how to share your faith the way Jesus did, don't miss these helpful resources:

God Has a Wonderful Plan for Your Life: The Myth of the Modern Message (our most important book).  This essential teaching, in a brief, easy-to-read book, is designed for anyone who wants to quickly learn how to share the gospel biblically.

Hell's Best Kept Secret and *True & False Conversion.* Listen to these vital messages free at LivingWaters.com.

How to Bring Your Children to Christ … & Keep Them There. These time- 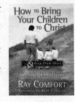 tested principles will help you guide your children to experience genuine salvation and avoid the pitfall of rebellion.

For additional resources and information about Ray Comfort's ministry, visit **www.LivingWaters.com**.

RAY COMFORT is the producer of "Audacity" and other award-winning movies, and has written over 80 books. He cohosts a TV show that airs in over 200 countries. He and his wife, Sue, live in Southern California.

JULIA ZWAYNE is a gifted young poet and novelist who loves God, and has a deep passion for overseas missions. She lives with her family in Southern California.